Dakota Sky

Ray Aman

Note for Librarians: a cataloguing record for this book that includes Dewey Decimal Classification and US Library of Congress numbers is available from the Library and Archives of Canada. The complete cataloguing record can be obtained from their online database at:
www.collectionscanada.ca/amicus/index-e.html
ISBN 1-4120-3566-X
Printed in Victoria, BC, Canada

Offices in Canada, USA, Ireland, UK and Spain
This book was published *on-demand* in cooperation with Trafford Publishing. On-demand publishing is a unique process and service of making a book available for retail sale to the public taking advantage of on-demand manufacturing and Internet marketing. On-demand publishing includes promotions, retail sales, manufacturing, order fulfilment, accounting and collecting royalties on behalf of the author.

Book sales for North America and international:
Trafford Publishing, 6E–2333 Government St.,
Victoria, BC v8т 4p4 CANADA
phone 250 383 6864 (toll-free 1 888 232 4444)
fax 250 383 6804; email to orders@trafford.com

Book sales in Europe:
Trafford Publishing (uk) Ltd., Enterprise House, Wistaston Road Business Centre,
Wistaston Road, Crewe, Cheshire cw2 7rp UNITED KINGDOM
phone 01270 251 396 (local rate 0845 230 9601)
facsimile 01270 254 983; orders.uk@trafford.com

Order online at:
www.trafford.com/robots/04-1394.html

10 9 8 7 6 5

Dakota Sky

This story is based on facts, personal experiences and impressions of life on the South Dakota prairie. The dying cottonwood tree on the cover of this book used to shade the windmill, water trough and separator house. Only a granary and outhouse remain of what once was the family farm.

About the Author

Ray Aman was born and raised on a farm in South Dakota. Vantage Press published his first novel, Revolution USA 2000, January 1997. A Lost Soul, his second writing is unpublished and in manuscript form. Dakota Sky was published by Trafford Publishing January 2005. He has resided in Colorado for the past forty-six years. Mr. Aman took up writing to express himself and stimulate his mind in retirement.

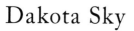

Dakota Sky

Chapter I

Thousands of years ago, buffalo, gophers, coyotes, hawks, eagles and other wildlife lived alone on the central prairies of North America. Later, those prairies became known as Indian Territory, and still later, Dakota Territory. Dakota is a name derived from the Lakota Indians who settled in with the wildlife on the prairies. The prairies also were known as the north central plains. Indians moved along streams and the mighty Missouri River, fishing and hunting big game, mostly buffalo. Different Indian tribes fought over hunting territories until the white man showed up on the prairies and their life changed forever. German-Russian immigrants arrived in the late 19th century and built sod houses, dug wells, plowed up buffalo grassland and built fences around their homesteads. The Plains Indians' nomadic way of life was no more.

The ruling class in Germany owned the land and employed common folks of the lower class to perform labor on farms in a semi-bondage status. The caste system existed in Germany and all over Europe. The Russian Czar invited Germans to farm rich, fertile land along the Black Sea. The Germans were promised freedom of religion and allowed to speak their language. Russia was a large country, sparsely populated, that the Czar aspired to develop like America. The Czar, like German princes, restricted landownership to a selected few, mostly the rich and powerful, like themselves.

Nikolai Lenin organized the Bolsheviks with intentions of overthrowing the Czar and putting in a utopian form of government. The original ideas for this new form of government that allowed equal participation of every citizen emanated from the writings of Karl Marx. The Czar was about to conscript German residents in Russia into his army to fend off the revolting Bolsheviks. The Germans were not interested in the Bolsheviks' revolution and had no desire to fight them in the Czar's army. German residents in Russia had a deep desire to own land. Russian revolutionists promised to turn ownership of everything over to the People's Republic, the new government.

During the late 1800s, the United States Cavalry had pushed the Sioux Indians to reservations, and the Dakota Territory was opened for homesteading. German-Russians made their way via ship from Russia to New York and by rail from New York to the Promised Land, Dakota Territory. The Milwaukee Railroad Company was eager to have the central plains settled by farmers and ranchers. The railroad paid ship passage for German-Russians from Russia to New York and provided free rail transportation from New York to the Dakota prairies.

The plan was to plow up the prairie and plant wheat, corn and other grains to expand the breadbasket of the United States. River bottomland was rich soil four feet deep that remained productive for many years. Hilly land covered with rocks that had only a few inches of black topsoil was, however, soon depleted in productivity. The rocky land should have been left in its native state as buffalo grass. This story is about hilly land covered with rocks located six miles northeast of Hosmer, South Dakota, homesteaded by the Schultz family.

Soon after Mr. and Mrs. Schultz, German-Russian immigrants, laid claim to their homestead, Dakota Territory was divided into two states, North Dakota and South Dakota. State, local and municipal governments were established. Counties and school districts were formed. The railroad spur off the Milwaukee Railroad in Roscoe stretched north to Strasburg, North Dakota. The spur rail line gave birth to towns like Hosmer, Hillsview and Eureka. Each town had a railroad depot, sidetrack for freight cars and a water tower to supply steam engines with water.

The Schultzes dug a shallow well and then built a one-bedroom sod house with straw and clay on their homestead. They plowed twenty acres of the 160-acre homestead with a sod-busting plow pulled by two oxen. Mr. Schultz sowed flax, wheat and some barley by hand. He carried the seed in a small sack under his left arm and spread seed with his right hand. In the fall, he cut the grain with a scythe and stacked it by hand with a pitchfork. A neighbor thrashed Schultz's grain crop with a horse-powered thrashing machine.

Homesteaders had to be self-sufficient to survive on the prairies from the outset, and that would not change for many generations. It was six miles to town over a bumpy wagon trail. Trips to town by ox-drawn wagon were limited to seasonal ventures. They had to visit the store in town for basics like salt, pepper, sugar, flour and cooking oil. They purchased farm tools and implements as income permitted. Sometimes, one neighbor bought various supplies for a group of neighbors on his trip to town.

The Schultzes built a shed for two oxen, two cows and a few chickens. The 160-acre homestead was established and destined to flourish. WWI created a great demand for farm products. The Schultzes made extra money in those years and invested in more cows, two teams of horses, better plows, a new drill to plant wheat and a cream separator. The pioneers had enough extra money to buy lumber for a new house and barn. The future looked promising for German-Russian homesteaders on the Dakota prairies.

Midwest America, from the Mexican border to the Canadian border, became a vast agricultural area. Wheat was raised and shipped to mills in Minneapolis; hogs were raised, fed and shipped to Chicago for slaughter. Cattle grazed on buffalo grass west of the Missouri River, and then were corn fed in Iowa and shipped to slaughterhouses in Chicago and Kansas City. Railroads hauled farm products produced on the prairies to Chicago, Minneapolis, St. Louis and Milwaukee. Manufactured goods were shipped by rail from those cities to consumers on the plains. The railroad was king during that era. A telegraph line, a single wire stretched on poles paralleling the railroad on railroad right-of-way, carried messages in and out of the plains.

Mr. and Mrs. Schultz had four children. Two, a son Jacob and a daughter Emma, lived past their first birthdays. Due to a complete lack of medical care, frontier life claimed the young and weak adults. The fittest, with a bit of luck, survived on the prairies.

Jacob married Catherine, a neighbor girl, so named after Catherine the Great of Russia. Catherine was of Russian and German ancestry. Some German men residing in Russia married Russian women. Jacob and Catherine Schultz were the second generation on the Schultz farm. Jacob bought more land, four more horses and new farm implements. One hundred acres of the original 160-acre homestead was pastureland. He expanded his herd of cattle, and with his father's financial help, he bought an abandoned 160-acre homestead of cultivated land adjacent to the Schultz farm.

Jacob and Catherine had four children. A son Carl and daughter Ruth survived the harsh prairie environment and reached adulthood. One of Jacob and Catherine's daughters was stillborn and the other lived only a week. They both were buried on the edge of the Schultz farmyard. Jacob and Catherine planted a cottonwood tree to shade the two little graves. The deaths of the two unnamed daughters were recorded on the front page of the family Bible. The Schultz family Bible served as the official record of all marriages, births and deaths.

Carl's parents, Jacob and Catherine Schultz, moved to town after Carl and Gertrude married. Carl and Gertrude became the third generation living on the original Schultz homestead on the Dakota prairie. Jacob and Catherine raised a garden and chickens in Hosmer. They didn't bother with a cow, a hog and pumpkin patch like some of the other retired farmers. Jacob and Catherine relied on their son Carl and his wife to provide them with cream, pork, beef and flour.

As an investment for their retirement, Jacob and Catherine bought eighty acres of land two miles south of the Schultz farm. The land was expected to produce annual revenue for them. Owning land was paramount to the German-Russian immigrants. Farmland was what they knew and loved. Raising wheat and farm animals was their way of life, the only life they knew. Carl expanded the farm by buying a 160-acre abandoned homestead of cultivated land and leasing 80 acres from his parents.

Jacob and Catherine deeded over their interest in the original Schultz homestead to their son Carl with the understanding that he look after them for the rest of their lives. Elders relied on their children for support as they aged. Prairie families took care of each other. The welfare system was years away but some day would wrap around farmers' lives like a blanket suffocating them.

In Hosmer, Jacob and Catherine Schultz were happily retired. They lived in a new house that they had built for them, with a horse-and-buggy barn, chicken coop and outhouse. Then, Jacob died suddenly from a massive heart attack. Catherine was devastated over his death. He was a relatively young man and had been in good health. They had been retired only two years when death struck him down. Catherine turned bitter and carried that bitterness with her to the very end. She felt that life had cheated her. Two of her babies were buried on the Schultz farm and her husband was buried at the Hosmer Cemetery. His death became another entry in the family Bible.

Gertrude gave birth to her first child in the Eureka Hospital on May 15, 1928. She was named Cathy, in honor of her grandmother, Catherine Schultz. This did little to cheer up Grandma Schultz. Her daughter Ruth had married a rancher, Paul McGregor. The McGregor ranch was located far away, west of the Missouri River. Ruth and Paul McGregor had a two-year-old son christened Jack McGregor. Grandma Schultz had never seen her grandson. She was not pleased that Ruth married a rancher and moved far away. She was thankful that her son Carl lived on the family farm just six miles from Hosmer.

Chapter II

On a cold, miserable, dark January morning in 1930, Gertrude was about to go into labor. A snowstorm had been blowing without stop for three days. Snowdrifts abounded everywhere, around buildings and across roads. Some snowbanks were six feet high, stretching across roads from fence line to fence line. Wind had blown snowdrifts so hard neither a horse nor a Ford Model T truck or Model A car could make it through. Carl couldn't make it to the only hospital in McPherson County at Eureka by himself and certainly not with a wife who was about to give birth. He faced a real dilemma. The neighborhood phone lines were not functioning; he couldn't call anyone for help. Carl resorted to the ways of his forefathers and set out on foot in search of a midwife. He replaced the batteries in his flashlight and walked in a blistering snowstorm along a fence line on a county roadway to the Schmidt place one mile east of the Schultz farm. Mrs. Schmidt had given birth to eight children herself and assisted other women in the neighborhood with childbirth. At about breakfast time, Gertrude gave birth to a boy. She had a difficult time in birthing. Mrs. Schmidt, the midwife, feared losing Gertrude and the boy. The birth was successful, but Gertrude would never have children again. Sometimes life on the Dakota prairies could be very harsh. Carl wrote into the family Bible, "Joseph Carl Schultz born on January 19, 1930."

The next day, the wind subsided and the sun came out to shine on a quiet and extremely cold day. The temperature had dipped to twenty-five below zero. It was time to dig out the snow at the entrances of the barn and chicken coop. The cattle and horses needed a load of hay to feed on, cows had to be milked, hogs needed to be fed and watered, and chickens had to be looked after. There was no water in the cattle's water tank; it was completely frozen and the water pump was frozen shut. A fierce wind blew out the water tank heater. Carl chopped ice away from the heater and lit the puddle of oil in the bottom of the heater. Excessive heating oil in the bottom of the burner exploded and flames shot up out the chimney. Carl then poured hot water from a teakettle to thaw out the water pump shaft and engaged the windmill. There was only a little breeze so he had to pump water by hand. He pumped water into a hole he had chopped out on the edge of the water tank so that cows and the horses could drink water two at a time. Later that afternoon, the water tank heater melted out most of the ice so that cattle and horses could finish drinking water. After Carl and Gertrude got the farm animals fed and watered, Carl set out to fix the phone line.

In a two-square-mile area, farmers strung a single heavy-gauge wire on top of telephone poles following the fence line on their property. This put neighboring farmers in touch with each other in a closed-circuit phone system. The phone system served its purpose, but with limitations. There was no phone connection to Hosmer and, therefore, they could not reach out beyond their little circle. The phone was powered by a "B" battery placed inside the phone box. There was a crank on the right side of the telephone and a hook for the receiver on the left side of the telephone. When the receiver was placed on the hook, it disconnected the current from the battery and that shut down the output of the phone. That didn't prevent neighbors from listening in on other folks' phone conversations. All they had to do was to remove the receiver after hearing one farmer calling another farmer and listen to the conversation, and sometimes even engage in that conversation. Different sets of rings were assigned to each farmer. The Schultzes had a short, long and a short ring assigned to them. Frequently, the phone system didn't function because some farmers didn't properly splice the phone line and thus caused a weak signal across the entire phone system. Some farmers let the phone wire sag to the ground or touch the barbed wire fence, and this caused a short in the system. Long-distance phone calls to other parts of the country had to be made in town at a local phone office. Telegraph messages were received and transmitted by railroad depot agents.

The road to Hosmer was improved sufficiently for the Model T Ford truck and Model A Ford car to travel across in good weather and dry conditions. After a heavy rain, the narrow dirt road became slick and treacherous. Many times it was impassable after a spring snowmelt or a downpour because the water level in lakes and sloughs rose above the roadway. On a particular Saturday evening, when the Schultzes were in town, a storm dumped two inches of rain in two hours. The road became impassable and they stayed in town with Grandma Schultz. Other folks drove up to where water crested the road and slept in their cars until daylight. They either drove across the muddy roads or abandoned the car and walked home with their groceries.

* * * * *

Carl and Gertrude Schultz were unaware of the consequences of the stock market crash of 1929. Too many people had been borrowing money from banks to invest in a rising stock market that soared in value by the hour. When the stock market crashed, investors' stock became worthless and they couldn't pay back their bank loans.

In 1933, Franklin Delano Roosevelt became president of the United States of America. His first priority was to make the banks solvent again. He declared a bank holiday. Banks canceled all bad loans on their books, confiscated depositors' savings and used that money to become solvent again.

Grandma Schultz lost her entire life's savings of $10,000 on the bank holiday. That was a crushing blow to her. She still had her house and the eighty acres of land that would provide her with an income. Carl and Gertrude supplied her with pork, beef, cream and flour. She insisted that Carl have barley and wheat rough ground for her flock of twenty chickens. Her garden, potato patch, chickens and Carl's food supply from the farm would be sufficient for her survival.

Grandma Schultz's well was a four-by-four hole in the ground about twelve feet down, boarded and boxed with wooden planks. The water was not potable. She pulled up water from the shallow well by a bucket attached to a rope that rolled across a pulley and used the water to irrigate her garden. The potato patch was left to the mercy of rainfall. Grandma collected rainwater in a wooden barrel as it drained from the roof of the house. She used the soft rainwater to wash her hair and take an occasional bath in a metal tub. Drinking water was available from a neighbor who had a deep well that was pumped by a very tall windmill.

Few people in town had indoor plumbing. Some folks drained their sewer water into a hole full of large rocks in the back of the house, a leach field of sorts. There were water lines throughout the town, but no sewer lines. An electric-generating unit powered by coal supplied a limited amount of electricity to residents and businesses in town. Grandma Schultz never had her house connected to city water or city electricity. She maintained a country lifestyle in the city.

Carl, on the other hand, a progressive man, installed a 32-volt electrical system on the farm that supplied electricity to the house, chicken coop, barn and his blacksmith shop.

Chapter III

In the year 1936, during the Great Depression, Joe turned six years of age and his sister Cathy was eight. Carl and Gertrude often talked about the good times of past years to their two children who had no memories of the past; they only knew the present. Cathy and Joe vicariously experienced their parents' difficulties of the present. The entire country was in the middle of a depression and the central plains were in a drought. It had not rained in four years. Dust storms and snowstorms plagued folks on the prairies. Grasshoppers, Russian thistles and wild sunflowers invaded the Dakotas.

President Roosevelt in his radio fireside chats attempted to assure citizens that better times are around the corner. He reminded Americans that there was "nothing to fear but fear itself" as soup lines in industrial cities became longer and longer. Farmers on the plains lost their land to banks on mortgage foreclosures and county property tax sales because of unpaid taxes. Banks and a few town folks who had money purchased foreclosed land.

FDR, as Franklin Delano Roosevelt became known, introduced many programs for unemployed workers and bankrupted farmers. Dakota farmers had many sons and no work for them. FDR instituted a work program called the Civilian Conservation Corps (CCC) that built lodges, dams and roads in national parks. Some young men joined the CCC, and others joined the Army. There were those who in idleness rode freight cars across the country and became bums. A descriptive slogan for them evolved: "Put another nickel on the drum for a bum." On a local level, FDR put the Work Progress Administration (WPA) into motion. The program provided money to improve county roads. A worker with a shovel was paid a dollar a day. Carl Schultz was paid $1.00 a day for driving his team of four horses hitched to a sloop and his team was paid $1.25 per day for pulling the sloop. Carl was disappointed that his team was paid twenty-five cents a day more than he received. In the mornings, he harnessed four horses, fed them some hay and oats, and then after breakfast gave them water. He hitched the two inside horses to a wagon, filled a twenty-gallon tank with water and scooped up oats in a five-gallon bucket for the horses and placed his lunch bucket and jug of water next to the horses' water and oats. Carl and his team of horses worked on a county road near the schoolhouse. The WPA workers moved dirt from the tops of hills down across culverts in sloughs to raise the roadway and prevent flooding after a heavy rain or spring melting snow. County roads were upgraded from a wagon trail to a passable road for cars like the Model A and Model T Fords.

The money Carl made working for the WPA with his team of horses and produce from Gertrude's garden, meat and eggs from chickens and milk from two cows kept the family from starving. He had to borrow money from a wealthy man to pay taxes on his and Grandma Schultz's land. There was nothing left to sell on the farm. Carl had sold all except four horses to the soap factory. He had to shoot and bury his hogs because they got sick with cholera. The government compensated him at market price for the hogs he killed. That put him out of the hog business. Gertrude was raising turkeys on the theory that they would feed on grasshoppers, and there were plenty of grasshoppers everywhere. She intended to sell turkeys for cash. Her project failed. Domestic turkeys are the dumbest bird on earth. During a heavy rain, they will drown themselves catching raindrops. Gertrude's two-dozen turkeys gathered in a corner of the empty hog barn on a hot August day and all but three suffocated. She butchered the three survivors and canned the meat. Carl had sold all of his cattle except for two cows and four heifers. Gertrude was milking the two cows and Carl shipped the four heifers to a dairy farm near Brookings, South Dakota. The heifers would be bred and milked at the dairy farm until the rains came again to the Schultz farm in McPherson County. The drought was not as severe in southeastern South Dakota as it was in the north central part of the state.

* * * * *

The Schultzes' neighbors, Fred Schmidt, his wife and children, didn't fare too well; they were at the very end of their means. Mrs. Schmidt had helped deliver little Joe Schultz into the world six years ago. The Schultz and Schmidt families maintained a close relationship throughout the years as neighbors. Their children attended Cleveland District #2 school and the parents visited each other frequently, playing cards, eating sunflower seeds and drinking homemade beer. The older Schmidt son played the accordion and his younger brother played the clarinet. The two provided entertainment when they were in the mood to play. Both boys were self-taught musicians. They listened to Lawrence Welk play music on the WNAX radio station in Yankton, South Dakota. The oldest son, twenty years of age, signed up with the CCC, and his younger brother, eighteen years old, joined the Army; that left six children at home. Fred Schmidt worked for the WPA on the same road project with Carl Schultz. Fred couldn't feed his family on county welfare and WPA wages. The bank foreclosed on his loan and repossessed his farm machinery. The county put up his land in a tax sale. He couldn't pay his taxes and was not in a position to borrow money. Mrs. Schmidt's two cows went dry; there was no more milk. Fred Schmidt took the last sack of wheat that was seed for the future when the rains would come again and had it ground up into flour. He still had four mangy-looking horses and his wife had a dozen chickens and her garden that supplied vegetables. Fred Schmidt was at the end of his rope, a euphuism that nearly came to pass. Mrs. Schmidt kept praying for her family, but to no avail.

Gertrude, Cathy and little Joe were collecting cow pies with a team of horses hitched to a wagon that had been left by cattle in the pasture from previous years. Cow pies and corncobs were used as kindle to ignite coals in the cooking stove every morning. The three had made their way almost a mile to the east along the southern fence line of the pasture when Cathy saw someone running toward them from the Schmidt farm. The east end of the Schultz's pasture was a quarter of a mile from the Schmidt's farm. Cathy said, "Look, Mom, someone is running this way." Gertrude said, "I think it's your friend Susan." Cathy Schultz and Susan Schmidt were the same age and best of friends in school; they were like sisters. It was Susan Schmidt running toward them crying.

Susan blurted out, "Mommy wants to move to California and Daddy wants to hang himself." In detail, she told the terrifying story of her father's attempt to hang himself from a rafter in the cow barn. She explained that he made a loop on the end of a rope, placed it over a beam and anchored the other end to the trough. He was going to stand on a three-legged milk stool, put the rope around his neck, kick the stool away and hang himself. Tears were streaming down her cheeks as she told the sordid story. When her dad got up on the milk stool, she said, "Daddy, don't do it. Please don't do it." He took the rope down and sat down on the milk stool and cried. She said, "We are so poor we don't know what to do."

Carl and Gertrude Schultz came to the aid of their neighbor. They spread the word that Fred Schmidt and his family needed money to move to California because they were down-and-out and had lost everything. Carl arranged for folks to deposit money into an account at the bank on behalf of Fred Schmidt. Mr. Schmidt, the proud man that he was, would never know who donated what to his cause. When the bank informed Fred of the donated money in an account for him, he sheepishly withdrew the money. Carl, Gertrude, Cathy and Joe made repeated trips to the Schmidt farm delivering jars of canned meat and vegetables for the long trip to California. Carl had wheat ground into flour for them. It was a bittersweet day when Fred Schmidt made his last phone call to Carl telling him that they were leaving early the next morning. Cathy and little Joe were completely engrossed with the Schmidt family's departure to California and Fred's attempted suicide. The two distraught children talked of nothing else from morning to night. Cathy left the door to her bedroom open and so did Joe. Joe was afraid to sleep by himself with the door closed to his bedroom. The two talked until one or the other fell asleep.

When the Schultz family arrived at the Schmidt farm the next morning to say their final good-byes, the Schmidts had their Model A Ford and Model T Ford truck loaded with boxed canned food, clothes, bedding and a few sticks of furniture. It was a sad scene. Fred, a defeated man, was venturing into an unknown world with his family against everyone's wishes. They didn't want to leave their home, and the Schultz family didn't want them to leave. It was either a move to California or to starve in South Dakota. Fred and his family were one of many families on the move. Most folks moved to California to pick fruit. Carl and Gertrude continued their daily routine of surviving and watching the Dakota sky for rain, but all they ever saw was grasshoppers on the move. At high noon the skies turned yellow with grasshoppers migrating north in the hot blazing sun. There wasn't much for the grasshoppers to chew on except thistles and wild sunflowers. Carl noticed that grasshoppers were chewing on fence posts and stripping paint off the west side of the house. Grasshoppers took a bite out off everything they landed on, even fabric. Carl had holes in his shirt made by nasty grasshoppers while he was wearing it. Grasshoppers bit holes into Gertrude's laundry as it dried on the wash line.

Out of desperation, Carl cut thistles and stacked them for the two cows and four horses to feed on in the winter months. Grass didn't grow for years during the drought, but thistles grew everywhere in abundance. Thistles tumbled against fences and collected dust that piled up three feet deep over the years. Thistles piled along fence lines like a snow fence. They caught snow in the winter and dust in the summer.

Carl mowed and raked green thistles into a pile for stacking. Thistles didn't rake well; they got hung up in the rake's teeth. With a fork, Carl pitched the thistles up on a pile and Gertrude with her pitchfork moved thistles to form a round stack. Cathy and little Joe stumped on the ball-like thistles to flatten them out and stay in place. Cathy and Joe complained because they had holes in the bottoms of their shoes and the thistles stung their tender feet. Gertrude put cardboard paper in the shoes as insoles. The thistle harvest was another project that ended up in futility, like Gertrude's flock of turkeys. The cows and horses didn't eat the thistles; they would rather starve than eat the thorny weeds. Carl set the thistle stacks on fire. They went up in a blaze within minutes.

Carl wanted to rid himself of two things, thistles and grasshoppers. He plowed a firebreak around an eighty-acre field and ignited thistles along the north end of the field with a burning oil-soaked rag. The fire raged twenty feet high and raced down the field at ten miles per hour burning thistles, grasshoppers and everything else in its path. In minutes, the eighty acres were blackened from the inferno, exposing rocks, pheasant nests and roasted grasshoppers. Pheasants fared well during the drought; they fed on grasshoppers and sipped water from the morning dew.

Saturday evenings were a treat for farmers; they gathered in Hosmer to socialize and buy the basics, sugar, coffee, salt, pepper and other items used in canning and curing food. Carl bought supplies for his blacksmith shop. From time to time, he needed welding rods and a tank of acetylene for his welder and cutting torch. Women gathered in the grocery store, creamery or drugstore. Men had many places to congregate: the car dealership, farm equipment dealer, blacksmith shop, elevator and the pool hall or saloon. Young men spent most of their time in pool halls drinking draft beer, chewing sunflower seeds and playing a game of snooker or eight-ball on the pool tables. The older fellows enjoyed draft beer and sunflower seeds likewise but preferred to play a game of cards like high-low-jack or pitch. Little Joe followed Cathy around town and patiently waited for his sister to stop at the drugstore for an ice cream cone, root beer and a sweet stick of licorice. Children and grown-ups visited along storefronts as they wandered around town. People would rehash Fred Schmidt's attempted hanging and discuss news of families in distant corners of the county that were leaving their drought-stricken farms. On the way home, Carl and Gertrude would chew salted store-bought sunflower seeds and spit the shells out through the car windows. Some of the shells would blow into the back seat, hitting Cathy and Joe in the face. The two children would chew gum and discuss their visits with old and new friends.

On Sunday mornings, they drove to the country German Reformed church one mile beyond the schoolhouse, the same road Carl had been working on with his team of horses. Carl explained that road improvements would permit year-around travel. He forgot to mention snow in the winter months. At church they met folks who shopped in Hillsview instead of Hosmer. These people knew neighbors who lived close to Leola, the county seat for McPherson County. Prevailing conversation centered on the drought and who had left their farms for California and those who were preparing to leave. After church services, Gertrude always walked to the small graveyard in back of the church where her father was buried. Her mother was still living with two sons on the family homestead a short distance to the east of the church. Gertrude was born on that farm. One Sunday, as the Schultz family got into their Model A Ford, a car was churning up a trail of dust traveling at a high speed toward the church. The driver was from the Leola area. Folks gathered around his car to hear him announce the suicide of a farmer four miles to the northeast beyond the church. The farmer's funeral was going to take place at the man's farm.

On the way home, Carl and Gertrude made plans to attend the funeral of a man they had seen on their trips to Leola attending to matters at the country courthouse. Carl said he had never met the man and only knew of him. Folks from far and near were curious to see this dead man's bullet hole. He shot himself with a 22-caliber rifle. The man who made the surprise announcement at the church of this man's suicide didn't know why the farmer killed himself. Cathy told Joe her version of the suicide with her personal embellishments. Cathy had a way of holding her little brother spellbound with her stories. She didn't know any more about the man's death than Joe did. Cathy, at eight years of age, two years older than Joe, acted like her brother's mentor. She had a good imagination and used it to the fullest. She had become a good storyteller practicing on her brother. Joe respected his older sister and believed every word she uttered.

The funeral turned into a social afternoon with folks congregating from miles away to satisfy their curiosity of the suicide. Most of the people at the funeral had never met the man. Cars were parked circling the farm buildings. People looked under the crabapple tree where the farmer laid down and shot himself in the right temple. There was a long line of folks leading into the house where the body was on display in a casket. They had come to see for themselves the bullet hole in the side of the dead man's head.

The funeral began as a social gathering and turned into a macabre experience when they moved the body from the house to a freshly dug grave under a cherry tree. The wife of the dead man wailed, cried and kept having fainting spells. Two strong men carried her in a chair from the house to the gravesite. Six farmers laid the man to rest in his grave facing toward the east. They pulled the rope up from around the casket and immediately shoveled dirt over him.

On the trip home, Cathy gave little Joe her version of the funeral. She made remarks about the tattered clothes some of the children wore and noted the worn-out shoes all scuffed up with holes in the soles and turned-up toes. Some boys had partial shoelaces strung through a few eyelets. Joe said that the boys looked funny to him. Gertrude explained from the front seat that folks at the funeral looked strange to him because he didn't know them. She said, "They are no different than us." After cresting a few hills in silence, Carl said, "Nobody seemed to know why he shot himself. The farm was in tiptop shape and he was doing as well and not any worse than other farmers." Gertrude said that she overheard some women say that his wife was crazy and drove him to suicide. The farmer's two teenaged children, a boy and a girl, showed no emotion at the funeral. They knew why their father killed himself and they knew their mother's state of mind, but said nothing.

The next morning, Carl harnessed up four horses and drove to the WPA project. Gertrude washed clothes with the gasoline-powered Maytag washing machine. Joe followed Cathy around as she did her chores. She fed the chickens and poured water into their trough and then watered a section of the garden. Cathy took her snare and a bottle of water and walked with Joe north of the farm to a prairie dog colony. She talked a blue streak telling Joe how she would snare gophers, cut off their tails and mail them to the county commissioners in Leola for a reward of three cents per tail. The gopher tail reward was her spending money.

Cathy put the loop of the snare inside a gopher hole and strung the line back about ten feet and lay down flat on the ground in wait for the gopher to emerge from his hole. She pulled the snare taut as she instructed Joe to lie next to her and be very quiet. Joe kept whispering to her about her next move when a gopher peeked out of his hole. Cathy said, "Just be quiet and watch me." Gophers were poking up from other holes that probably were all connected underground within the colony. Cathy was looking about the colony when Joe said, "There he is." Cathy jerked on the snare, and the gopher leaped up out of the hole. Then she pulled him in, put her foot on his body, opened her pocketknife, grabbed the gopher's tail with one hand and cut off his tail with her pocketknife. She took her foot off the gopher and let him jump out of the snare. He ran off and ducked into a different hole. Joe yelled, "You didn't kill him." Cathy said, "All I wanted was his tail. It's worth three cents."

* * * * *

Saturday was a welcome day for Cathy and Joe as they made preparations for the evening. The two enthusiastically did chores early and took a shower in the separator house by the windmill before supper. Carl and Gertrude showered after supper. Carl mounted a thirty-gallon tank on top of the separator house with a garden sprayer head for a showerhead. Water heated in the tank from the hot sun during the day. After Cathy and Joe took their shower, Gertrude refilled the half empty tank with cold water. Water heated up in time for Carl and Gertrude's shower. On rainy days they took cold showers.

They always stopped at Grandma Schultz's house before driving into town. She talked up a storm during their weekly visits. Grandma got very lonesome living by herself. It was difficult for Carl and his family to say goodbye to her and head into town for the evening.

Gertrude bought sugar, coca and vinegar and a few other staple items for her bare pantry. She also bought cloth for dresses for herself and Cathy. She picked up a pair of corduroy pants for Joe that she couldn't resist. Cathy and Joe wandered up and down the sidewalk checking out folks seated on benches in front of stores. The drugstore was their favorite spot where they bought a 5-cent ice-cream cone, a one-cent licorice stick and a 5-cent root beer. A youngster in the Dirty Thirties could buy a lot of happiness with fifteen cents. Carl discovered that a local feed and seed store was handing out free grasshopper poison by courtesy of the federal government. Carl picked up his allotment of two sacks and placed them between the front fenders and the hood of the Model A Ford. The car had no trunk. Instructions were furnished on how to spread the poison. Carl glanced over drawings that showed how to build a spreader. The instructions didn't present a problem for Carl. He had lots of scrap iron and a well-equipped blacksmith shop to build the spreader. He was so encouraged with the idea of poisoning grasshoppers that he visited his favorite pool hall. He bought a package of salted sunflower seeds, a glass of draft beer and got into a game of high-low-jack. He felt lucky and hoped to win twenty-five cents to pay for his treats.

On Sunday morning, Carl set out to build the spreader with a 40-gallon barrel with a shaft that extended through the barrel from top to bottom and attached to a disc with fingers welded inside the disc. The disc rotated from the motion of a trailer tire.

Carl didn't have a rubber tire trailer. He only had wagons with steel-rimmed wooden wheels, so he removed the right rear fender of the Model T truck and mounted the spreader against the truck box. It took Carl a week working evenings to build the spreader and mount it onto the truck box. Gertrude drove the truck and Carl fed poison into the barrel as they spread poison along a section line on the west 160 acres. The next day he had to flush out grasshoppers that were sucked into the radiator by the cooling fan. He placed a screen across the radiator to keep grasshoppers from getting lodged in the coils. Grasshoppers were everywhere in a multitude beyond imagination.

A week later, Carl checked to see the results of the grass-hopper poison. He walked the fence on the 160 acres and found many dead grasshoppers. There were more hoppers now than before he and Gertrude spread the poison. He was very dismayed.

Fall was approaching and that meant Gertrude would do a lot of canning, thanks to a bountiful garden. The garden was watered with well water that overflowed from the cattle and horse water tank. The windmill pumped cold water up from thirty feet underground to the surface into a 55-gallon barrel and overflowed into the cattle and horse water tank. Inside the 55-gallon barrel, Carl bracketed a ten-gallon cream can that served as a cooling compartment for the butter and cream. He put the beer into water surrounding the cream can. Watermelons floated in cool water in the cattle and horse water tank. Water overflowed from the cattle water tank into a large pipe that flowed downhill to the garden.

Gertrude canned beets, watermelons, cucumbers, carrots and beans. She had a crock for cabbage. Popcorn, garlic and onions were tied in bunches and hung up in the potato cellar. Gertrude's garden was a lifesaver for the Schultz family. During the summer they enjoyed fresh carrots, scallions, lettuce, radishes, peas and potatoes.

They had two cows. One needed to be bred by the neighbor's bull so she would give birth to a calf and provide milk again. After two years, the calf would become a young heifer or steer and make for a fresh supply of beef. The only beef left was a few jars that Gertrude had canned two years ago.

This fall Joe started his first year in school. He and Cathy walked to school across their pasture and a short distance beyond over a neighbor's pasture to the schoolhouse. They carried water in an empty wine bottle, an egg sandwich and an occasional molasses cookie with their books in a homemade school bag. In October, WPA work ended for the season and Sam, their riding horse, became available for Cathy and Joe to ride. Sam was a tall, strong reddish-brown horse with a white diamond between his eyes. He was a very gentle horse. Cathy had practiced riding him around the barnyard. Carl had to teach her how to ride Sam with Joe seated behind her holding on. If they fell off or had to dismount Sam, they had very little chance of getting back up on him. Most likely, they would have to walk home leading Sam by the reins. Carl and the other school board members had built a four-stall horse barn at the school. A pond below the schoolhouse was to be Sam's drinking water, but because of the drought, there was no water in the pond until the rains came again. Sam had to do without water all day. During the winter he munched on snow. Carl had placed some hay in a corner stall of the horse barn.

In early November, Carl told Gertrude they were running short of the wheat he had been saving for seed when the rains returned. He questioned Gertrude feeding the chickens any more wheat. That day Carl took a sack of wheat to town and had it ground up at the flourmill.

Carl had lost all hope. He knew that the end was near. He fell into complete despair. That evening after supper, he walked to the west side of the summer kitchen and watched the sun set on 160 acres that had produced only thistles for the past four years and was infested with grasshoppers. Cathy and little Joe stood at his side and watched him cry. They had never seen their dad cry before, and that experience was to remain with the children forever.

* * * * *

The next morning, Carl fed Sam some oats, bridled him and led him to the water tank for a good drink. He hoisted Cathy and then Joe upon Sam and turned them loose. With Cathy's urging, Sam headed out to the county road and off to school. Sam knew the route to school very well. From the time they arrived at the school grounds, they stopped speaking German and it was English-only. It was forbidden for children to speak German during school hours on school grounds. All the children at school spoke broken English. German-Russian children were taught basic subjects in school: arithmetic, reading, writing and speaking in English. Cathy was a good student and became Joe's tutor.

Carl spoke very little that morning. The stress of the times got to him. He strung up a rope across the beam in Sam's stall in the barn and placed a three-legged milk stool at the bottom of the loop of the rope that was anchored to

Sam's trough. He went to his sanctum sanctorum, the black-smith shop, closed the door and sat down in semi-darkness to cogitate his demise.

In the afternoon, Sam came marching into the barnyard with Cathy and Joe on board. Sam was thirsty because he had not had a drink all day. He headed straight for the water tank. Carl or Gertrude was not around to assist the children in dismounting Sam. Cathy was a creative thinker. She rode Sam behind the hay wagon and helped Joe slip off Sam and step on the wagon; Cathy did the same. Leading Sam by the reins, the two walked over to the barn and pushed open the door. Cathy saw the rope dangling above the milk stool in Sam's stall. She screamed. Sam snorted and turned around to leave. Gertrude abandoned collecting eggs in the chicken coop and ran to the barn. She was stunned at the sight of preparations for a hanging. Without speaking a word, she dismantled the hanging rope and methodically took the bridle off Sam and fed him some oats. She said to Cathy, "Go up to the hayloft and put down some hay for Sam."They left the barn door open for Sam so he could leave his stall after finishing his oats and wander around the barnyard for the night. He liked to roll back and forth on the ground to rub his back.

That evening, Gertrude did her best at the supper table to cheer up everybody. It was a scary experience for Cathy and Joe that afternoon. That night in bed, Joe talked from his room to Cathy about the hanging rope they found in Sam's stall until she no longer answered. When he realized that she had fallen asleep, he rolled over and cried himself to sleep whispering, "Daddy, don't die. Daddy, don't leave." Carl didn't speak to anyone for two days. He just kept everything to himself. On Saturday evening, Cathy and Joe were anxious to make the trip to town, but Carl and Gertrude didn't show any inclination to go. Cathy knew not to talk about the trip to town with her mother under the circumstances.

Gertrude talked Carl into attending church on Sunday morning. They drove to Hosmer and took Grandma Schultz to church with them. Gertrude knew Grandma Schultz would communicate with her son. The two had the deepest respect for each other. After the church service, Grandma Schultz insisted that they visit her husband's grave like she did every Sunday. The visit to the cemetery and Grandma's Sunday dinner of chicken and dumplings brought Carl back to communicate with his family again.

On Monday morning, Cathy and Joe rode to school on Sam, Gertrude did the laundry and Carl busied himself in the blacksmith shop. He took a hard steel tooth of a hay rake, heated it on his homemade forge until the steel turned red, yellow, almost white, and then hammered the steel flat on an anvil into the shape of a butcher knife. He started the single piston engine that rotated a long shaft with pulleys on it that powered the grinder, press drill, and formerly the forge fan. He ground it sharp and riveted a wooden handle to the knife. Carl was an innovative man in his blacksmith shop. He rewired a six-volt generator to run on the 32-volt power system and then shaped fins and soldered them to a pulley that fit to the motor shaft. He used a coffee can to make the housing for a blower. He used an empty five-gallon oilcan for a hood and connected a four-inch pipe to it and vented smoke and fumes from the forge through the roof. That was Carl's homemade forge. His next project was to build a rubber tire trailer to replace a wobbly, high wooden wheel steel-rimmed wagon.

Drought, grasshoppers, thistles and dust storms that blocked out the sun in midday were daily reminders during the Dust Bowl days that life on the farm could end any season. Carl worried over losing the farm because of unpaid taxes or a bank foreclosure. These things preyed on his mind and became a burden that he no longer could bear. He discussed with Gertrude borrowing money from a businessman in town to pay property taxes on their and Grandma's land. They were in arrears on taxes owed to the county, and if they didn't pay back taxes this year, they would lose the farm at a county tax sale.

After a lunch that was black coffee and a slice of bread with syrup spread on it, Gertrude took the boiling hog fat and lye mixture and poured it into a wooden box to form soap bars. She made her own soap to do laundry and bought bar soap for bathing when she had the money. That afternoon she ground up horseradish, put it into small jars, added some vinegar and put a cover on the jar. She also did some canning that afternoon. She was forever canning and preserving something for the long winter months. When she didn't trust the rubber-sealing rings that provided a seal on the rim of a jar and the cover, she melted wax and poured it on top to seal the contents at the neck of the jar. She reused the wax many times. Carl and Gertrude survived by their wits; almost everything was homegrown or homemade. They made their beer and capped it in empty ketchup bottles. In better times, Carl bought a pint of 180-proof grain alcohol, mixed it with burnt sugar and added anise and peppermint for flavoring. That recipe was Carl Schultz's homemade schnapps. The Dirty Thirties were the worst of times that brought the best forth from the German-Russians on the Dakota prairies.

* * * * *

The 1938 winter came upon the prairie like most winters did in South Dakota, mercifully cold and windy. Enough snow fell for northwest winds to form six-foot drifts over county roads, closing them to travel for weeks at a time. Carl had hauled enough coal to the schoolhouse, his house and to Grandma's house to last into spring. They wouldn't freeze to death this winter. Carl decided to take advantage of the cold winter. He and Gertrude dug a 10x10-foot hole six feet deep by the garden that fall. As the freezing weather came along, on a breezy day he put the windmill to work and pumped water into the hole and let it freeze layer by layer. When the hole was a block of ice within two feet below ground level, he covered the large block of ice with straw. The straw was insulation to keep the ice from melting during the summer. Carl planned on having ice available all summer from his buried block of ice.

They were low on pork and beef, so Carl came up with an inexpensive way to provide meat. He ordered 25 pounds of herring. Winter cold temperatures kept the fish frozen in a rail car. The Milwaukee Railroad brought freight and mail to Roscoe and from thereon a train running on the spur line up to Hosmer and beyond to Strasburg, North Dakota. The railroad was the lifeline into the prairies. Everything came in and went out by rail.

If a big package or box of live chicks was due for delivery, the mailman called ahead to inform the farmer in the morning of the delivery. The farmer waited patiently by his mailbox on a county road for the mail carrier. The mailman was very dependable on his deliveries. Muddy roads sometimes kept him from making his rounds, but snow didn't bother him. He came up with an ingenious vehicle to traverse snow on county roads. He adapted a Model A Ford car into a half-track, or it could have been called an original homemade snowmobile. On the front he mounted two snow runners between the two front wheels. When he approached a snow-bank, he lowered the runners so the front wheels lifted up and the weight of the car rested on the snow runners. On the rear of the car, he placed a second set of wheels in tandem and double-chained both wheels to make a rear-tract drive like that of a caterpillar tract. After crossing a snowbank, he raised the snow runners and drove down the frozen dirt road on the two front wheels and the rear halftrack.

* * * * *

In 1938 a week before Christmas, a northwest storm blew in and dropped a foot of snow. Things were looking up. Carl thought maybe, just maybe, sloughs and lakes would be wet enough from winter snowstorms to produce hay in lakes and maybe he could seed wheat and barley in low areas bordering sloughs. The county road was closed in both directions because of snow. Cathy and Joe were displeased because it meant a Christmas listening to the radio and scanning the Sears Roebuck catalog for a wish list that wouldn't materialize. Carl set out to save Christmas for the family.

He hitched Sam and his teammate to the sled and prepared for a cross-country trip to the German Reformed church a mile beyond the schoolhouse. On Christmas Eve, under a bright moon and in a breathless freezing night, Carl guided the team across snow and frozen ground. Joe was cold despite a heavy horse blanket over him and his mother cuddling him. Half way in the trip, Joe started to complain; he wanted to get off the bumpy sled and walk home. Sled runners screeched as they slid over hard windblown drifts. On some drifts the sled moved sideways. The sled was used around the farm to skid heavy things around and was not adapted for passenger travel. Gertrude and the children sat on the flatbed of the sled; Carl drove the team standing up. Joe had another reason for not wanting to make this trip. He had neglected to memorize the Christmas verse assigned to him. He lost his desire for a brown paper bag of nuts, hard candy, and an orange and maybe a Mars or Milky Way candy bar.

They arrived at the church half frozen and stiff. Sam and his mate bellowed steam from their nostrils. Carl unhitched the horses and tied them to the sled. Gertrude and the children stiffly made their way into church. Body heat and an inadequate coal stove had not warmed up the church. After Carl and two other men finished lighting all the little candles placed on branches of an evergreen tree, the church heated up immediately. The tree looked like it was ablaze. It was a scary sight. Carl suggested that they blow out the candles less they burn down the church. The service started by singing a favorite German Christmas song, O Tannenbaum, to the accompaniment of an out-of-tune organ. The minister brushed over the Christmas story in German. The German language in the German Reformed Church was considered the holy language. The minister moved to the heart of the Christmas program, recitals by the children. Cathy was the fifth child called upon for the recital of a verse in front of the congregation. After a few more recitals they sang Silent Night. Little Joe nervously told his mother that he had to pee. He went out around the corner of the church toward the outhouse and stopped at a spot where others had taken a pee and did his business. He then returned to the church porch and waited until he heard his name called. Carl responded and said that Joe was outside. The minister moved on to the next name on his list. Joe slowly made his way back to the bench where Cathy and his mother were seated. Gertrude scowled at him. She suspected that Joe schemed his way out of reciting the assigned Bible verse. The Christmas service ended with the singing of Oh Little Town of Bethlehem, and then brown paper bags with peanuts, walnuts, cashews, hard candy, an orange and a Milky Way bar were passed out to every child. The brown paper bag of nuts was the only gift children received this Christmas. Carl hitched up Sam and his teammate to the sled and they bounced, bumped and slid on toward home. Joe was so cold and tired he didn't know if he was dreaming or slowly freezing to death.

On Christmas morning, Carl and Gertrude surprised their children. They had splurged on a small telescope for Joe and two books for Cathy. Cathy hugged her books with all her might. Joe had wanted a telescope for months. He had stopped looking at telescopes in catalogs. The boy had given up all hope of receiving a Christmas gift. Joe's friend had told him that with a telescope he could look through one hill. Cathy and her mother explained to him how a telescope works and how it didn't make it possible to look through or over a hill. Gertrude was filled with gratitude to have put joy into her children's lives on this holy day.

During these dire times, folks living on the prairies expected very little in pleasures and learned to do without many necessities. Carl was saddened that they couldn't spend Christmas with Grandma Schultz. Gertrude said to Carl, "She walked to church and was with friends." Gertrude was kidding herself. Grandma probably went to church by herself and went home the same way. She had few friends in Hosmer.

Carl tuned the radio to WNAX in Yankton to hear President Roosevelt's holiday message to the American people. FDR said that the country was coming out of the Depression soon. He encouraged Americans to hang in and expect better times around the corner. After the president's short pep talk, Lawrence Welk played his accordion while leading his band in German waltzes and polkas.

* * * * *

Carl built an incubator to hatch chicks for Gertrude. He placed a panel of light bulbs for heat over a shallow box of fine sand. Eggs rested in sand heated by light bulbs. The incubator was a short-lived creation. Out of sixty eggs only fifteen hatched. He blamed the fluctuation of power from his 32-volt electrical system for the failed hatch and Gertrude blamed inbreeding. Another Carl Schultz creation went down in failure.

Gertrude had not infused her flock with new chicks in recent years because of the Depression. Their cash flow was a mere notch above starvation. The best she could do was to trade a couple of roosters with a neighbor and strengthen the bloodline of her flock. She said to Carl, "I will let the hens nest behind the chicken coop. Let them do the hatching for me." Some hens answered nature's call in spring by building a nest in a grove of trees and lilac bushes behind the chicken coop and hatched their eggs. After the hatch, the mother hen led her half-dozen chicks to the front of the chicken coop and showed them where the water and food were. Gertrude put ground wheat out for the little chicks.

Her flock of chickens ate many juicy grasshoppers for there was an abundant supply of hoppers.

* * * * *

Spring melted snow and water flowed into sloughs and dry lakebeds. Carl was encouraged to see water flowing again but that was short-lived like all hopes and prayers of past seasons. Green grass that grew in the low-lying areas quickly dried up in the heat. It didn't rain and Carl went back to work on county road projects with his team of horses. WPA wages for him and his team were the saving grace for the family. Carl's personal moneylender in town promised not to foreclose on him. The lender believed that better times were around the corner like FDR had said in his radio address. Carl told Gertrude he didn't want to attend church anymore because prayer was all in vain. The long duration of the drought made Carl cynical.

Gertrude suggested he get some ice from his ice pit and make some ice cream. He said, "Okay, but first I want to show Joe how to tease a rooster." He tied a piece of black thread around a kernel of corn and tossed it toward an old but not so wise rooster. When the rooster made a move toward the kernel of corn, Carl yanked it away and the rooster drove his beak into the ground. Joe and Cathy enjoyed Carl's sadistic game with the rooster. Gertrude said, "Stop that and get some ice."

Ice in the pit had melted down a few feet despite the straw on top for insulation. Carl put down a short eight-foot ladder and with a hayfork and ice pick in hand made his way down the ladder into the ice pit and commenced to remove the straw on top of the ice. He saw a couple of garden snakes slither away under the straw. He pulled straw away from the dirt walls and saw about thirty snakes in one corner. Without hesitation he scampered up the ladder and out of the snake pit. He immediately shoveled dirt into the hole and covered up the snakes. Another of Carl's grand ideas disintegrated before his eyes.

On Saturday evening they drove to Hosmer. Acres and acres of farm machinery on the outskirts of town that had been repossessed by the bank provoked Carl. The sight of machinery that once belonged to farmers who now were picking fruit in California turned him bitter. Their first stop was at Grandma Schultz's house. They dropped off butter, a butchered chicken and milk. Grandma was thankful to her son and his family for the help. Her bitterness over the bank confiscating $10,000, all of her savings, showed and Carl sympathized with her.

Cathy and Joe still had some gopher-tail money left for treats at the drugstore. Joe licking on his chocolate ice-cream cone said to Cathy, "I am glad Dad covered up those snakes. I don't like snakes." Cathy agreed, "I wouldn't eat ice cream made with snake ice." Joe and Cathy's bedroom-to-bedroom conversation that night was about snakes in the ice pit. Cathy fell asleep before Joe and snored through the night. Joe had snake nightmares.

* * * * *

Nothing seemed to change from year to year. Carl looked up past the blacksmith roof and saw a yellow sky at mid noon, grasshoppers on the move. He had bought a Ford Model T truck from the bank that had been repossessed from a farmer. Carl was building a heavy-duty rubber tire hay wagon for use when the rains came again. Building the trailer was more of an exercise in retaining his sanity than the immediate need for a rubber tire hay wagon. He disassembled the truck down to the frame, axle and wheels saving all the other parts of the truck for his metal junk pile next to the blacksmith shop. He made metal chisels from valve stems and a sundry of things with odds and ends from his junk pile. Carl was a very creative guy in the blacksmith shop.

When dust storms darkened skies in midday, Gertrude turned on lights in the summer kitchen and house. She didn't bother to dust around the house anymore; she scooped up dirt an inch deep from windowsills and placed wet rags around edges of the windows. Gertrude was depressed much like Carl. Watering the garden and hoeing weeds kept her mind in balance. Working in the dirt and growing food was good mental therapy. Produce from the garden became weaker, and some plants completely failed because Gertrude didn't have the money to buy new, hearty seeds annually. One cow went dry in the spring and the other showed signs of going dry. Lunch again would be coffee without milk or sugar and syrup on a slice of bread.

Carl bridled up Sam and drove the dry cow up the road a mile and a half to Herman's farm to let his bull service Gertrude's cow. Herman didn't charge Carl for the bull's service. He said, "That lazy bull of mine needs a workout." Herman had a great sense of humor even in these difficult times.

Carl continued to work for the WPA with his team of horses. He hitched them up in the morning, loaded water and feed for them into the wagon and placed his lunch and water jug next to the horses' rations. Cathy and Joe walked to school because Sam was part of the four-horse team working on the county road.

Gertrude brought in the laundry from the wash line and made supper. She treated the family to chicken and dumplings with natural gravy. The children came home from school and rushed into the kitchen. They could smell supper cooking a distance from the house. Carl came home with his team. He unhitched the horses, fed them and turned them loose for the night. There was some short grass around the sloughs that they nibbled on before sunset and then they laid down and rested for the night. Carl washed up and sat down to listen to WNAX on the radio. Lawrence Welk and his band played waltzes and polkas for German-Russians on the Great Plains. Lawrence was born and raised near Strasburg, North Dakota. He didn't learn to speak English until he was 21 years old. He was one of the plains people. At 6 p.m. FDR was going to give another one of his fireside chats. Carl said, "I wonder what that socialist has on his mind tonight." Gertrude chimed in, "Maybe he has some good news for us. Things are going to get better. This may be the last year of grasshoppers, thistles and dust storms." She hoped that chicken and dumplings and Lawrence Welk music would cheer Carl up. Intuitively, she thought that they had lived though the worst of times. Carl, on the other hand, was still pessimistic and grew ever more bitter.

Roosevelt gave his speech and America listened. He said that Europe was coming out of a depression and that would affect American industry in a positive way. He warned the country of a dictator named Adolph Hitler who was gearing up for war. FDR said that Hitler wanted to conquer all of Europe. German-Russians on the plains had more faith in Hitler than in Roosevelt. The WNAX announcer said that industries in Chicago, St. Louis, Minneapolis, Milwaukee and Detroit thought that the Midwest would rise out of the Depression next year. Folks on the plains were affected by the Depression and drought both at the same time. A bumper crop without a market for wheat, barley, pork and beef could be as bad as a demand for livestock and grain but no rain to grow them.

On weekends Carl rebuilt the engine in the 15/30 International tractor. He put in new piston rings, took sleeves out of piston connecting rods to take up slack and cleaned the block and head of the engine. He did the same to the Model T truck and Model A car engine. He bought two more old cars from the bank's repossessed equipment yard and made two more tire-wheeled trailers to replace the old horse-drawn wagons. He modified a 3-bottom 14-inch horse plow with a hitch to fit to the drawbar of the tractor. Carl became so engrossed in rebuilding farm equipment that his pessimism slowly grew in optimism.

Joe asked Cathy about good times that he overheard his parents talk about lately. At the age of eight years he only knew life as it was today and had few memories of yesterday. Cathy took secondhand knowledge from her mother and embellished it with her imagination for Joe. School started in September and the two children carried on many discussions, half in German and half in the English language, on their trek to school. When they reached the school grounds they made sure to speak only English since German was forbidden. Most German-Russians spoke German at home and attempted English in town and slipped in German words for terms that they couldn't express in English.

On the way home from school, Cathy sometimes deviated from the direct route diagonally across the pasture to cover different sections of the pasture and scout for new gopher colonies. Gopher tail money was a more reliable source of spending money than dependence on a handout from parents. Fall came and Carl stopped working for the WPA. Cathy and Joe were happy to ride on Sam to school. Cathy said that Sam preferred going to school every day than pulling dad's scoop with his three teammates all day long on the county road project.

Chapter IV

After another cold, windy Dakota winter in 1939, rains finally came in the spring. Snowmelt put water into sloughs and lakes and rain greened fields. All indications were that the drought was over. It was sheer pleasure for Carl to burn thistles and grasshoppers along fence lines. Gertrude asked Carl to return her four cows from Brookings. She wanted to sell cream again, raise calves and rebuild the herd. In the fall, Carl sold his first wheat crop in years, a small one, and paid off the personal loan he owed to his wealthy friend in town. When he paid off the loan, his friend said, "I knew you were good for the money, Carl." Carl felt good about himself for the first time in years. He was out of debt but didn't have cash on hand to expand the farm. He enthusiastically related all this to his mother, Grandma Schultz. She said to her son, "I got money." She went up the attic of her house and came back down carrying a gallon syrup can full of bills, $500 in all. She said to Carl, "You take and buy cows and more horses." Carl was dumbfounded. She went on, "Make the farm big again." Carl had no idea that his mother had squirreled away this much money.

Herman, his lifelong friend to the north, was retiring. His two daughters had moved to Minneapolis, leaving him and his wife alone on the farm. There was a market for his livestock and land so he sold out and retired. Carl bought Herman's six cows, four horses and two pregnant sows. Carl bought new seed for the spring planting and encouraged Gertrude to order new seed for the garden and rejuvenate her flock of chickens with three dozen Leghorn chicks. She bought two geese and four ducks from Herman's wife.

Grass grew where once only thistles and wild sunflowers took root. Crop yield was high because cultivated fields had been idle for years. Carl and Gertrude were thankful that they endured the Dirty Thirties, the Dust Bowl Days. The Schultz family celebrated, Carl made his schnapps and Gertrude bought new clothes for Cathy and Joe. The two children were on the brink of experiencing what their parents meant by "the good old times."

The mailman called from Hillsview and said that a box of chicks came in that morning by train and he would be delivering them to their mailbox around 11 a.m. At 10:30, Gertrude drove the mile up to the mailbox and waited in the Model A for the mailman. She checked the box for dead chicks; there were only two out of thirty-six. The chicks chirping on the trip back to the farm was music to Gertrude's ears. She had told Carl at breakfast that they needed to buy a white-faced bull without horns from the McGregors. Carl answered, "We'll do that this fall. Now we'll seed all the land

and have a bumper crop this fall. Make money. Then we will buy a bull, new car and maybe a new tractor."

Carl plowed fields with the 15/30 tractor from dawn to dusk. Gertrude harrowed and seeded the plowed land with a team of four horses, rotating them every other day. Cathy and Joe had their assigned duties before school in the morning and in the evening after school. Joe put feed out for the chickens, ducks and geese, then put water out for them and collected eggs from nests in the chicken coop. Cathy did work around the house and an hour before sunset she started milking cows. Gertrude helped Cathy finish milking after she tended to the horses. Gertrude turned the cream separator by hand and Cathy fed the calves their evening ration of milk. At dusk Carl came home from plowing in the Model T truck. He slopped the hogs and then refilled gasoline cans for the tractor and refilled grease guns and oil cans to lubricate machinery. They all washed up, ate supper and went to bed. It was a long day of hard labor for every member of the family, but a happy one. Working for the WPA was a means of survival, and working the land was the real life on the Dakota prairies.

* * * * *

Carl assembled a crew to thrash his crop and three neighbors' crops. Labor was no problem in 1939; there were idle farm boys looking for work by the dozens. Carl was making money from his bumper crop and thrashing his neighbors' crops. Gertrude nearly wore out the Sears and Roebuck catalog ordering clothes for the family. Carl bought a new car, 1940 Plymouth, and made plans for the long trip to west river country to buy a white-faced bull, without horns. Horned cows and bulls were not welcome in the Schultz herd; they tended to gore each other if not dehorned. Carl and Gertrude left Cathy and Joe behind to tend to the animals while they were on a long trip across the Missouri River to the McGregor ranch. They left instructions with Cathy to call a neighbor if a problem arose. Animals on the farm needed to be looked after twice a day. Cathy and Joe could do all the chores easily except milking the cows in the morning and evening. Joe haphazardly milked two young cows and Cathy had to pull the teats on six older cows that gave out a lot of milk. They skipped school for two days and managed the farm. Carl and Gertrude returned in the old Model T Ford truck with a beautiful young white-faced bull. Carl vowed to buy a bigger, better truck next year. The Model T served him well but couldn't haul big loads and the engine was underpowered. He needed a bigger truck with a stronger engine.

Gertrude was full of news about Paul, Ruth and Jack McGregor. She told Cathy and Joe that their cousin Jack was a good-looking tall cowboy, who some day will own the 6,000-acre family ranch. She said that he wins prize money riding broncos in rodeos.

This fall was different from years past. After they stacked the fall cutting of hay, they thrashed crops and then picked corn by hand until Thanksgiving. Gertrude had her potato cellar full with pumpkins, popcorn, potatoes, squash, onions, garlic and horseradish, and the cellar beneath the house was full with crocks of cabbage, canned tomatoes, melons, pickles, carrots and beets. She didn't grow rice or navy beans; she bought them at the store. Carl had money in the bank and no longer needed to make his own wine and beer. However, he preferred his homemade schnapps to the store-bought. Gertrude still patched clothes, sewed aprons, and made bedding with the down from geese and ducks she butchered. One of her great pleasures was buying nice clothes for her children. She bought corduroy knee pants with suspenders for Joe. Joe reluctantly wore them. At the age of nine, he preferred to wear long pants held up by a fancy belt.

Every level of government had money and so did its citizens. McPherson County built up main roads leading to Hosmer, Hillsview, Eureka and Leola, the county seat. They placed a layer of gravel on the six-mile road to Hosmer from the Schultz farm, and that was a welcome blessing. FDR still made his speeches to the country. He sought reelection again. Some of his jump-start New Deal programs were still in effect and others were abandoned because they didn't work. WPA and make-work programs for unemployed men were no longer needed. Roosevelt was talking about the coming war in Europe. Farmers on the plains who survived the Depression and Dust Bowl Days were too busy farming and making money to concern themselves with international politics.

Numerous New Deal programs that subsidized Midwest farmers for planting limited acres or compensated farmers to plow under excess crops were instituted to regulate fluctuating supply. Some farmers were marginal and sub-marginal operators who failed despite Agricultural Adjustment Act, Civil Works Administration programs and other "make-work" programs. The Commodity Credit Corporation extended loans for crops kept in storage and off the market. This was another attempt to control supply to meet demand. The Soil Conservation Service taught farmers to reduce soil erosion by crop rotation and to plant trees to create wind shelterbelts. These programs were the beginning of the end of "laissez-faire" on the prairies. The federal government commenced to compensate sub-marginal and marginal farmers to leave their cultivated land idle. The theory was to keep the farmer from moving to town and going on welfare. Despite various programs to save unsuccessful farmers, many folded and moved to town in search of more security. Subsidized programs by the federal government put wheat farmers on a permanent welfare system. Carl never signed up for any of President Roosevelt's New Deal programs. He was a risk-taker. Carl worked WPA because he wanted to support his family without government welfare.

Carl bought another eighty acres of land to the south-west of his farm and set out to make more and more money. He wanted to farm all the land he could. Carl was a farmer who avoided government interference and survived on the Dakota prairie living by the "laissez-faire" philosophy.

Gertrude bought a propane gas-cooking stove and talked Carl into letting her have a new Maytag washer powered by an electric motor. The motor rotated the agitator and powered a wet-clothes ringer. She and Carl bought a small electric refrigerator to keep cream and butter from spoiling. Gertrude needed modern conveniences to allow her more time to work in the fields. Life changed for everyone in the Schultz family with rains blessing wheat fields and pasture-land. Cathy and Joe were busy with chores and no longer had the time or found a need to snare gophers for spending money. Collecting cow chips for the kitchen stove was a thing of the past. They both wore nice store-bought clothes and new shoes. One pair of dress shoes for Sunday, tennis shoes for school and a pair of high-top leatherwork shoes. Grandma Schultz's life remained pretty much the same as always. She tended to her garden, cooked for herself, did her laundry and walked across town to church every Sunday, stopping off at the cemetery on her return trip home. By the summer of 1941, the Depression had become a memory, not forgotten, but a memory overshadowed by good times.

Roosevelt tried to prepare the Congress of the United States of America to enter the war in Europe. America was not interested in fighting a war. Industry geared up to satisfy past pent-up demand and to supply England with armaments. Farmers on the Dakota prairies didn't want a war. They wanted to live the good life. On December 7, 1941, Japan bombed Pearl Harbor in Hawaii. Everything abruptly changed and life would never be the same.

Chapter V

The United States of America was at war, World War II. The country was in the process of pulling itself out of the ten-year Depression and drought on the prairies with personal sacrifices flowing in their wake. The war would come with a heavy price for military personnel and a monetary gain with a few hardships for others on the home front. Farm boys signed up for military service by the droves. It was the right thing to do at the time. They had no idea what lay ahead in the months and years to come. Enlisting in the Army was an instant moment of glory for the naïve farm boy.

Volunteering for military service gave men the opportunity to belong to something with national pride. As a soldier, he would leave behind a family of eight brothers and sisters, who had shared beds and used an outhouse for a toilet and who left the dinner table hungry many times. His worn overhauls were replaced with brand-new khakis, a field jacket, cap, gloves and combat boots. Aside from his suntan uniform, everything was the Army olive green color. He wore brass designating the branch of service he was in and a patch indicating the unit he was assigned to. The farm boy turned soldier became a hero in the eyes of his family.

As a soldier, he slept in his own bed with clean sheets provided weekly. The mess hall was never short on food for the troops. The great reward at the end of the day was a nice hot shower. Indoor plumbing was a new experience. At the end of the month, he was paid in cash, brand new crisp bills. He had his picture taken at the Post Exchange (PX) in his uniform and mailed it home with a letter to his family and maybe to a girlfriend. Every GI had to have a girlfriend to brag about to his buddies in the barracks.

Carl, like most Americans, was slow to envision how war would change his life. He didn't buy a new tractor but he did buy a new four-door Plymouth car. He didn't anticipate that no cars or tractors would be manufactured until the end of the war. Industry went into producing Jeeps, Army six-by-six trucks, tanks, rifles, fighter planes, bombers, battleships, submarines, clothes and K rations (field chow) for servicemen.

Carl didn't have to worry about being drafted into military service because he was exempted as a farmer. Women were not subject to the draft, and men who were classified 4-F sought employment in factories. Uncle Sam needed fighting men on the military front and farmers and factory workers on the home front.

Carl's abundant labor supply vanished almost overnight. Johnny Hoffman was the only young man from his previous thrashing crew who was still around. Johnny was the last son left on the farm. His two older brothers had been in CCC camps and were inducted into the Army right after Pearl Harbor Day, December 7, 1941. His other two brothers signed up before the draft board gave them notice to report for a physical examination. Johnny's older sister went to Minneapolis and found a good-paying factory job manufacturing uniforms for Army troops. Johnny was exempted from military service when he turned eighteen years of age because he was the only son on the Hoffman farm. Likewise, Joe Schultz's cousin Black Jack was not drafted into military service because he was the only son of a rancher. The government needed fighting men and they had to be supplied with food, clothing and ammunition.

It was ironic how the same things that plagued Gertrude during the Dust Bowl Days surfaced again during the war, however, in a different manner. Nearly everything that was not grown or produced on the farm was rationed, like sugar, shoes, gasoline and tires. Other things that were not rationed disappeared from the marketplace for the duration of the war. Carl made use of Sam and two draft teams to circumvent gasoline rationing. Horses lived on grass, hay and grain. The tractor ran on gasoline. It was a dichotomy that during the Great Depression the Schultzes were dirt poor and couldn't afford to buy anything beyond bare necessities, and now they were making money hand over fist and couldn't spend any of it. They bought War Bonds to finance Roosevelt's war, World War II. Local perception was that Roosevelt went to war with Hitler and the Emperor of Japan to pull the country out of an economic slump.

German-Russians on the Great Plains of the Dakotas were in agreement with "der Fuhrer" of Germany at the beginning of World War II. They rationalized that Jews were the main problem in Europe and wanted Adolf Hitler to make Germany the central power in Europe. When mothers one by one hung up a banner with a silver star in their living room window signifying that a son was killed in combat on the front lines in Europe, attitudes toward Hitler and Germany in general changed dramatically on the Dakota prairie.

Carl worked from sunrise to sunset and sometimes into the darkness of the night. Gertrude and Cathy each worked a team of four horses harrowing, drilling and disking while Carl plowed field after field with the 15/30 International tractor. In the fall, he came up with a scheme to do the thrashing without an abundant supply of labor. Shortage of field hands was every farmer's dilemma. On a Saturday evening in town, Carl discussed his plan to overcome the problem of labor shortage with his neighboring farmers. The "Carl Schultz Plan" required his neighbors to group together as a thrashing crew. They would move from one farm to the other and do the thrashing themselves. The farmer whose wheat was thrashed hauled the grain to his sheds on the farm or trucked it to a town elevator and sold the grain for cash. Wives and daughters did the cooking for the thrashing crew. Carl was paid a certain fee for every bushel thrashed. This worked out to the satisfaction of everyone. Four out of five farmers didn't have a thrashing machine or tractor to propel a thrasher. Joe, being too young to pitch bundles of wheat stacks, became Carl's assistant. He oiled the pulleys and chain drives on the thrashing machine. Thrashing hours were hard on Joe who was only twelve years old. He had to get up in the morning before sunrise and didn't return home for his shower until sunset. He was too tired to discuss anything with his sister Cathy at bedtime. His life became part of the thrashing crew from dawn to dusk. All meals were eaten at the farms where they were thrashing: breakfast, lunch, noon meal, afternoon sandwich and supper, the meal at the end of the day.

* * * * *

Winter came and spring arrived on schedule. Cathy and Joe relied more on the Model A Ford than Sam for a ride to school. When the dirt road became slippery after a heavy rain or was blocked off by snowdrifts, they rode Sam across the pasture to school or walked the distance to and from school. Carl preferred that Cathy and Joe drive the car to school allowing more time for them to do chores on the farm. Carl was obsessed to accomplish as much as possible with his merged crew of wife and two teenage children. The farm was Carl's top priority in life. Nothing else mattered.

He became obsessed with making money and enlarging the Schultz farm.

In spring, life on the farm became long days of working in the fields and added chores for Cathy and Joe. Upon the return from school, Cathy started milking the cows and Joe fed the hogs then the chickens. He collected eggs from the hens' nests and then joined Cathy in milking. He was a slow and reluctant stripper of cow teats. He hated milking cows. While milking cows, Joe and Cathy talked back and forth exchanging stories, opinions and ideas. Joe had turned thirteen that January and started to mouth his dislike for life on the Schultz farm. Cathy attempted to counter his notions of leaving after high school. She kept their conversations private. Cathy shared secrets with her mother and less intimate matters with Joe. Joe, on the other hand, kept certain thoughts to himself and shared almost nothing with his father.

Gertrude left the fields with her team of horses about an hour before sunset. She unharnessed the horses and turned them loose to pasture for the night. She helped to finish milking the cows and then ran the milk through a separator. Joe fed skimmed milk to the calves, Cathy washed up the separator and her mother put supper on the stove.

As darkness fell, Carl came home in the old Model T Ford truck, leaving the tractor in the field. The old truck was an amazing machine. It produced electricity from magnets on the flywheel. This provided current to the coils that sent a charge to each of the four spark plugs. The magnets produced electrical current for the headlights, although it was a very weak beam of light. Carl kept a flashlight in the toolbox under the passenger's seat for additional light if needed.

At sunrise Joe went in search of the horses and cows in the pasture with about six handfuls of ground oats in a paper bag that enticed Sam. The other horses either ignored Joe or toddled off a short distance, but Sam loved his oats and never failed Joe. He let Sam eat the oats and held on to his halter. After Sam finished the oats, Joe put a bridle on Sam and looked for a large boulder or a fence line where he could vault himself onto Sam. Sam was a tall horse. After he mounted Sam, he headed the horses in the direction of the farm and then crested a hill or two in search of the cows.

Carl had specific chores assigned to everyone in the family. He organized everything, including himself, in minute detail. The morning routine called for Gertrude and Cathy to milk the cows while Joe fed the animals and Carl harnessed the horses and invariably had to fix machinery at the blacksmith shop. One machine or another was always breaking down because they were old and worn out. Carl welded and patched up old equipment throughout the entire Depression and war years.

During the evening meal, Carl reviewed the day's accomplishments and failures, seldom complimenting anyone. He was prone to criticize his wife and children in a blunt, demeaning manner. According to Carl, there was only one way, the right way and that was his way. Perfection rested entirely within himself. Years later, his rigid ways would haunt him.

* * * * *

On July 4th Carl allowed the family to celebrate Independence Day, but not before certain chores had been done. He moved manure from inside the cow barn and spread it outside in front of the barn in a plot throughout the winter months. With a flat spade, Cathy cut small blocks of manure and Joe set them on end to dry out. The dried manure replaced cow pies that they didn't collect from the cow pasture anymore. Corncobs, pages from the Sears catalog, blocks of dried manure all served as kindling to ignite coal in a stove. In the absence of kindling, Gertrude would spill kerosene on coals to ignite them. It was dangerous to do this because it created fumes in the stove and could cause an explosion. Joe learned that lesson the hard way one cold winter morning. The wind had blown out the flame in the water tank heater and heating oil dripped into the boiler of the water tank heater all night long. Joe dropped a match into the puddle of oil in the bottom of the heater and nothing happened. He rolled up a page from the Sears catalog and lit it and then dropped it into the heater. It exploded into his face. Flames flashed across his wool stocking cap and singed his eyebrows. Joe didn't have eyebrows for the rest of the winter.

The only hard wood available came from old farm implements and was used as charcoal in the smoke house. Hams, pork sausage, pork shoulders and beef summer sausage were cured by a low heat and smoke from pieces of hardwood. A building next to the main house, called "the summer kitchen," served as a deep freezer in the winter. Carl managed well with his 32-volt electrical system he installed in 1930 but it didn't have enough charge to run freezers and numerous electric motors. If the wind was blowing hard, the three-blade wind charger could keep Gertrude's Maytag churning but couldn't keep up with Carl's welder. When he did welding in the blacksmith shop, he started up the gasoline-powered 32-volt generator. The Rural Electrification Administration (REA) that eventually electrified farmers on the plains was still ten years away.

A local grocery store in town installed a large walk-in freezer with cages that were rented out to customers, and this solved freezer problems for farmers. Farmers continued to butcher their own steers and hogs. They brought sides of beef and pork to the grocery butcher to have it cut up, wrapped and placed into a rented cage in the walk-in freezer. Gertrude bought wieners, luncheon meat and other cold cuts from the meat department at the grocery store. She made sandwiches with store-bought baloney and cheese. They washed down the sandwiches with cold bottles of Miller's beer for lunch that they ate out in the field. Carl and Gertrude didn't make home-brew and bottle it in catsup bottles anymore.

When Joe and Cathy were nearly finished cutting manure blocks, a robust heifer charged around the corner of the cow barn and butted Cathy to the ground. The heifer was aroused by the red shirt Cathy so proudly wore. With quick thinking, Joe ran into the barn and grabbed a three-prong bundle fork and stuck the prongs into the heifer's rump as she was about to roll Cathy against the barn wall. The heifer backed away with blood squirting from punctured holes in her butt. Cathy howled with fright and had tears streaming down her cheeks. Gertrude came rushing from the garden when she heard the commotion. Cathy explained to her mother what had happened as Gertrude comforted her with a hug. Joe was filled with pride when Cathy told her mother how he poked the heifer with a pitchfork. It had always been Cathy who looked after her little brother when the two were off by themselves. Riding to school on Sam, Cathy sat in the front with Joe behind holding on to her. The two looked after each other faithfully.

One time riding through the neighbor's yard on the way to school, the neighbor's dog barked and attempted to nip Sam's hind legs. Sam reared sideways and started to gallop up the rocky hill, and this excited the dog even more. Joe yelled to Cathy, "Stop. I am getting off." Cathy stopped Sam and turned him toward the dog. The dog snapped at Sam's other rear leg, and Joe pursued the dog with a swift kick in the butt. The dog squealed and made off to the farmhouse. Cathy rode Sam up to a large rock and let Joe leap up and seat himself behind her. The two laid out their strategy for the next day. Joe would dismount below the rocky hill and walk alongside of Sam. The nasty dog showed up and did his usual barking at Sam. When he was within range, Joe took one of three throwing rocks out of his pocket and hit the dog on the head and with the second rock hit the dog on his side. The dog yipped all the way up the hill back to the farmhouse.

Gertrude said to Joe, "After you finish with the manure blocks, go feed the hogs some slop and then wash up and change clothes. We are going to town for the Fourth of July." Joe heard the train whistle and steam puffing from the train on its way up from Hosmer to Hillsview, a four-mile distance from the farm. They couldn't see the train from the farm but could hear it chugging along on a quiet day. On cold, calm winter days, they could see a plume of steam rising from the train engine.

Joe scooped slop mash that was barley, corn and water from a 55-gallon wooden barrel. A piglet gulped down the mush and turned its head sideways, tumbled and fell to the ground. Joe was perplexed. He took a whiff of the mush as he put the cover back over the barrel. It smelled like his dad's grain alcohol. He concluded that the piglet got drunk on the fermenting mash. He had seen older boys stagger around the back of the pool hall after they had taken too many swigs of gin from a pint bottle on Saturday evenings. The family took turns showering in the separator house and then changed clothes and drove to town for the Fourth of July celebration. And what a celebration it turned out to be for Joe.

Joe lined up for the twelve-year-old foot race and won twenty-five cents finishing first. He entered the next race for boys fourteen years of age and under and again sprayed gravel from the starting point to the end of the race, coming in third and winning fifteen cents. Joe was neither twelve nor fourteen years old, he was thirteen, but nobody questioned him so he ran in two age groups. He was thirsty for a Nehi root beer after having run his races. At the drugstore, he bragged how he could drink a twelve-ounce bottle of root beer in one gulp. A city slicker he didn't know overheard him and said, "I bet you five cents that I can drink this bottle of Nehi orange faster than you can drink that root beer." Joe took him up on the challenge and made a quick nickel. On hot afternoons out in the field during harvesting, Joe poured water down his throat without taking a breath and that way learned the trick of pouring liquid down his throat without taking a swallow. The city boy didn't like having been beaten by a dumb farm boy who smelled of manure. Joe felt like a rich winner.

Cathy and her friends came into the drugstore for a vanilla ice-cream cone. She saw Joe and said, "We are going to the Ferris wheel. Do you want to come along?" Joe shrugged his shoulders and said, "Naw." He didn't think the Ferris wheel would be much of a thrill for him. On the farm he climbed up the windmill to grease the gears many times and strapped himself to the three-blade wind charger numerous times. Climbing the wind charger tower was scary. After the Ferris wheel ride, Cathy and her friends took a ride on a swing that spun them around in a circle. This ride was more fun for her than swinging on an old tire suspended by a rope from the cottonwood tree between the garden and windmill on the farm. However, swinging under the oak tree gave Cathy mental therapy. Joe asked what she was thinking about when she swung back and forth. She said, "Just thinking."

Cathy and her friends dismounted from the swing ride and asked Joe if he wanted to see a soldier. They went to a room behind the hardware store and there was a guy in a soldier's uniform lying on a bed. He had passed out from drinking too much whiskey. On their way home, Gertrude told Cathy and Joe all about that soldier they saw in town. She said, "He got a sixteen-year-old girl pregnant and then joined the CCC, and when war broke out, he was one of the first to go." Gertrude used the soldier as a way to lecture Cathy and Joe on sex before marriage. She said, "Joe, don't get a girl pregnant until you are married." Cathy listened and held her tongue. Grandma Schultz had told Cathy that she was born seven months after Carl and Gertrude were married. She went on and implied that if Carl had not gotten Gertrude pregnant, he could have gone on in school and become a lawyer. She said, "But, Carl rode around the neighborhood in winter playing cards and in summer played baseball every weekend and then he had to get married."

The sun was dipping low in the west as they drove home from the Fourth of July celebration. Carl veered into a small ridge of gravel that had been bladed to the side of the road. He had had a few drinks at the town saloon and was getting drowsy. He jerked the steering wheel to the right and sprayed gravel as the car fish-tailed. Gertrude elbowed him and said, "Ach! Mein Gott. Watch where you are going. Should I drive?" Carl regained his composure and drove the rest of the way home safely. Cows had come in from the pasture and were waiting by the water tank to be milked. Farm chores were always waiting to be done.

* * * * *

President Roosevelt asked that everybody collect scrap metal and old tires for the war effort. Scrap metal was chopped up and put into bombs; old tires and inner tubes were repossessed to make new tires. Joe and Cathy hitched Sam and his teammate to a wagon and collected everything in ditches along the farm property line. Scrap iron and discarded rubber were spending money for the two. Carl dismantled old farm machinery and sold it to the junk dealer in town. The bank's acres of repossessed old farm machinery on the edge of town disappeared almost overnight; it went into the war effort. The countryside was the cleanest it had been since the first settlers arrived in Dakota Territory.

Freight cars loaded with scrap iron and old tires rolled and rattled east to Detroit and other destinations daily. Trains pulled flatbed cars loaded with jeeps, army trucks, tanks and artillery guns to the west coast. Troop trains carried soldiers in the same direction. General Douglas MacArthur needed equipment and troops to fight the war in the Pacific.

Rationing on the home front was a constant reminder of the ongoing war. Farmers didn't concern themselves with meat, poultry and dairy products because they raised their own hogs, chickens, steers, and milk cows. Gertrude sold eggs and cream to her friends in town on the sly. She would leave eggs and cream on her friends' back porches on Saturday evenings. She was into the black market but didn't see it that way. She said, "Just helping my friends." Gertrude had to abide the rationing of shoes, sugar and coffee.

Carl was concerned about his gasoline allotment for the farm. Gasoline was tightly rationed. He used horses on the farm; they ate hay and didn't need gasoline. Tires were hard to come by. Tires wore thin and cracked open, exposing inner tubes. Carl patched inner tubes and placed boots inside tires to hold the inflated tube within the tire. When he was lucky enough to get a new tire for the truck or car, he took the used tire and put it on a trailer.

Gertrude was patching clothes because of war shortages. During the Great Depression, she mended every piece of clothing for the family several times because they were poor. Now they had money, but because of rationing and war shortages, some things were not available in stores, so Gertrude had to improvise.

Chapter VI

Fall came and it was time to reap the fruits of labor on the Schultz farm. Carl wanted to assign Cathy and Joe to a bundle wagon as an addition to the thrashing crew, but Gertrude wouldn't have it. She said, "They are too young. I will take a wagon with them." The farm and making more money was all Carl could see through his tunnel vision. He kept Cathy and Joe out of school until thrashing was finished.

Cathy was about to experience a big change in her life; she would start high school this fall and leave her brother Joe on the farm without her. He would ride Sam to the country school by himself for the first time. Cathy drove the Model A Ford to town until winter set in and then stayed with Grandma Schultz until spring. Grandma was getting along in years and no longer could stoke the coal furnace in the basement and carry coal upstairs for the kitchen stove. Cathy carried water from the neighbors to the house for kitchen use and bathing. Grandma Schultz avoided electricity, running water and sewer service from the town. She lived in the past in many ways, still hating the bank and Roosevelt for stealing her savings of $10,000 on that fatal bank holiday.

Cathy had good grades despite missing school in the fall for the thrashing season. Carl had his children's future all planned without their input. He said to Gertrude, "Cathy will go to Northern State Teachers College in Aberdeen and teach in a county school and Joe will stay on the farm." Gertrude added, "But Joe will go to high school." Carl didn't discuss his son's future schooling any further with her. In his mind, he owned the children and possessed all rights to his wife. Carl was sorry that his wife couldn't give birth to more children after Joe was born. He wanted a larger work force to expand the farm.

Carl's command was absolute and all had to obey. Gertrude had sworn at their wedding to love and obey Carl for the rest of her life, and she did that religiously. Joe tolerated his father with hidden resentment. The gap between father and son grew wider every day. Gertrude sensed this and tried her best to keep Joe from drifting away from his father.

Cathy fared much better with her dad than Joe did. She catered to him in ways that Joe could not and would not. She was confirmed in the German Reformed Church according to her dad's wishes. She memorized the Heidelberg Catechism in German and learned to sing German songs. Grandma Schultz taught her how to write in German. This pleased her grandma and her dad very much. Every year confirmation classes drifted from the German language to English in Bible and catechism studies. Carl considered the German

Reformed Church infallible, and the use of the German language made the church more sacred. He was adamant that none of his children ever marry a Catholic.

Carl, Gertrude, Joe and with the help of Cathy on weekends moved a barn from a 160-acre homestead Carl had bought. They took all the planks and boards of the old barn and built a garage for the Plymouth, truck and a new tractor. He had been promised a Model (M) International tractor in the spring. The new tractor would be a giant step up from his 15/30 International steel-wheeled tractor. The new tractor would have rubber tires, a power-take-off on the rear and an electrical system to power headlights and an engine starter.

* * * * *

Cathy brought Grandma Schultz out to the farm for Thanksgiving. Time spent on the family farm was exhilarating and stimulating for Grandma. She never adapted to life in town. Gertrude cooked a stuffed duck to everyone's delight. She told Joe to shoot a couple of pheasants for another meal. She said to Joe, "Don't shoot pheasants with that old shotgun; too much lead in the breasts." The pheasant population exploded by leaps and bounds. Grass and weeds along fence lines, roadway ditches and sloughs provided good coverage for nesting and protection against inclement weather and predators. Feed for the pheasant was plentiful around cultivated fields.

Cathy drove the Model A Ford down section lines looking to spot a pheasant head in grass on the right side of the car. Joe sat on the right fender of the car cradling the 22-caliber rifle across the hood of the car, looking for pheasants on the left fence line. When they spotted a pheasant, Cathy stopped the car and Joe paused for the pheasant to freeze and then shot him in the head.

During Christmas vacation, Grandma joined the Schultz family on the farm. Gertrude cooked a stuffed goose for Christmas. Goose and duck fat were revered in Gertrude's kitchen. She used the fat sparingly to glaze bread dough and in baking cookies.

* * * * *

January rolled across the Dakota prairies with a vengeance. It turned very cold and snow fell for days. The northwesterly wind drifted snow around buildings and across county roads five feet high. Mail was sometimes limited to one delivery a week.

Joe rode Sam every day across pastureland through the neighbor's yard and then a short distance to the schoolhouse. He put Sam into the barn and then fetched coal from the coal bin for the potbelly stove in the schoolhouse. At noon he put out a little hay for Sam. Sam desired Joe's attention more than the hay. At about 3:30 p.m., Joe bridled Sam and mounted him from a large rock at the corner of the horse barn and headed for home. Sam always trotted the first portion of the trip home. He was anxious for a drink of water and the ground oats Joe fed him in the barn. Sam was a happy horse. He was Joe's best friend.

The following morning another snowstorm drifted in from the north across the prairies. At breakfast Joe saw that the snow was coming down so heavy that visibility was poor. He said to his dad, "If wind comes up, this could become a very bad storm." Carl told him not to worry. He said, "If a bad storm comes along, hang on to Sam and let him bring you home. If you should fall off, keep walking until you reach a fence line and follow that back to the farm." He explained to Joe that a person walking in a blinding snowstorm tends to walk in a wide circle. Carl's instructions didn't encourage Joe but rather put more doubt and fear into his mind. Before breakfast, Joe dressed and went to the barn and fed Sam a ground-up barley and oats mix.

Gertrude didn't want Joe to ride off into the heavy snowfall. Carl insisted that Joe attend school every day during winter months because he missed so much school helping with harvesting and spring planting. Then Carl threw a barb at his wife, "You want him to go to high school, don't you?" Carl had an answer for everything. He seemed infallible. Gertrude packed a peanut butter sandwich, a pear and chocolate cookie into Joe's school bag. Joe filled a small bottle with water and put it into the school bag with the sandwich and reluctantly walked to the barn. He bridled Sam, let him have a drink of water and rode off to school.

It wasn't much of a school day. The one-room schoolhouse didn't warm up until about 11 a.m. After lunch, the farmer, where the schoolteacher took room and board, arrived with his sled and team of horses. He came for his two daughters and the schoolmarm. Joe bridled Sam and went on the ride of his life.

He dismounted at the neighbor's gate, opened and then closed it, stepped up on the second strand of barbwire by a fence post and pulled himself on Sam's back. The next fence separated another neighbor's pasture and the Schultz pasture. The three strands of barbed wires were pinned to the ground between two posts. Sam stepped across the wires and headed into the blinding snowstorm. Sam marched along at a good pace. Joe looked back to see the fence he and Sam had just crossed and all he could see was snow swirling. Fright set in. Joe didn't know how Sam would find his way home. There was little visibility. He could only see about thirty yards in any direction. His hands got cold. Wind blew up his pant leg and stung through his long johns. He tied the reins together and let Sam find his own way. His dad had told him to do that. He tucked his hands under his overcoat and braced himself against the northwest wind. Sam stumbled slightly and Joe almost slid off. This really scared him. He leaned forward on Sam's mane and put his hands around his neck. He knew that if he fell off and Sam should wander away in the storm, he surely would freeze to death. Joe's mind wandered. He thought of the little piglet that crossed by the hog barn and got hung up on a woven wire hog fence. It had gone down on its front legs in exhaustion and froze solid in that position. It was 30 below zero that night.

Joe panicked. He kept worrying about what he would do if he fell off Sam. He was not to lead him or else confuse Sam in the storm. Joe looked around and saw that blowing snow filled in Sam's tracks within seconds. He realized that he could not follow in Sam's tracks. Sam kept on walking at a good pace. The wind blew harder and he noticed that there was no snow on the ground. Joe figured that they must be on top of a hill. He saw a path by a fence corner but couldn't tell what part of the pasture they were in. He was sliding forward on Sam's back. He assumed that they were going downhill and that was why he was sliding forward on Sam. The pasture was hilly and had two ponds and a small lake on it.

Joe got dizzy from the swirling snow and complete whiteness. He felt sick to his stomach. Sam kept on walking up a hill, down a hill, through a snowbank and up another hill. Sam shook ice from his head and blew through his nostrils. Joe thought Sam said that everything was okay. Sam was icing up around the eyes and his nostrils.

It seemed like he had been riding for an eternity. He lost track of time and there was no visible reference to his location in the pasture. He knew he would freeze to death on this day. His mind drifted to the two most important people in his life, his mother and sister. His father insisted that he attend school today. He became angry and hated his father more than ever.

Sam slipped and slid. Joe grabbed his mane and hung on in fright. He knew that Sam was on ice, probably on the south end of the big lake. Sam went down on his hind legs and did a little dance and regained his balance. Sam leaped from the ice into a snowbank. It was like a buck. Joe clutched around Sam's neck as he stumbled though snow that came up to his belly. Sam struggled from the snowbank and walked up a slope. Joe took a deep breath and sighed in relief. He figured that Sam had taken the straight route toward the farm and crossed the southern edge of the big lake. Joe rode Sam on this route every day during the winter but never crossed the frozen lake. He thought he knew for the first time where they were in the pasture. Joe concluded that they were going uphill west of the lake and were a short distance from the farm. He sensed a descending motion and assumed that they were on the last hill east of the farm. The wind subsided momentarily. Joe noticed to his right a fence corner with a cow path around it that looked familiar. He couldn't see too well because ice covered his eyes and impaired his vision. He took off his right glove and pulled ice from his right eye. A gust of wind almost blew him off Sam. He lunged forward reaching for Sam's mane and dropped his right glove. He started to cry. Joe was falling apart emotionally. Sam snorted and shook ice from his head. Joe thought Sam was talking to him. He stuck his right hand in his coat pocket and hung on to Sam's mane with his gloved left hand. He could tell that they had reached the bottom of a hill. Sam shook his head back and forth. Joe's leg rubbed against a red barn door. Sam stopped. Joe recognized the sliding door on the barn. He caught a glimpse of the cattle water tank as the wind blew in gusts. He slid off Sam. They were home. They had made it.

Joe tried to lead Sam to the cattle water tank for a drink of water but he refused. Sam wanted to go inside the barn to his stall and eat ground oats and barley. Joe gave Sam three helpings of barley and oats and then went up to the hayloft and forked down the greenest, sweetest smelling hay from the stack and put it into Sam's feeding rack. He peeked around the corner of the barn and saw yellow between gusts of the storm. It was the house. He took off running toward the small gate on a fence between the barn and house. He made a mad dash for the house. His mother was waiting for him when he reached the house. She said, "You made it home." Carl looked at him, then Gertrude and said, "I told you Sam would find the way home." He took off his overcoat, untied the earflaps on the cap and hung it up over the coat. He sat on a chair without a backrest and removed his overshoes. He remained seated for a while to collect his thoughts. He realized that he was home. He hadn't frozen to death. Joe wanted to get up and hug his mother out of joy but didn't because the Schultz family didn't hug. Hugging was a sign of weakness. Shaking hands was a show of strength.

Gertrude fixed Joe a cup of hot tea with lots of honey. He was sipping his tea when his dad said, "I am going to do chores. Are you going to help me?" Joe stared at the wall across the kitchen table and didn't acknowledge his dad. Gertrude said to Carl, "Let him be. He had a hard day. Can't you see that?" The next day, he told his mother the horrifying story of the ride in a blinding snowstorm but didn't mention any of it to his father.

Next morning the wind had subsided. The Dakota sky was clear blue and the temperature was twenty below zero. Gertrude took it upon herself to let Joe stay home from school. It was his birthday. She told him that the storm yesterday reminded her of the day he was born. Carl decided to haul hay and manure because he had Joe to help him. Life to Carl was work, work, and do more work for the good of the Schultz farm.

Carl harnessed up two horses and hitched them to the manure spreader. By the time Carl drove out to the field, the wet manure froze to the floor of the spreader. They had to back the manure spreader into the cow barn and thaw the load of manure from the spreader box and unload it another day. They pitched hay into a wagon and then pitched it from the wagon into a large hayrack in the middle of the corral that fed the cattle and horses. They were pitching the second load of hay when Joe uncovered a brown ball in the haystack. It was a gopher hibernating. He was frozen solid. He wanted to bury the gopher in another haystack but Carl insisted that they thaw him out. Carl placed the gopher into a cardboard box and placed it by the kitchen stove. The next day the gopher thawed and died. When Carl made a mistake or goofed up badly, nobody in the family had the courage to correct him for fear of causing him to anger.

The train was on time. It was past noon. The train was midway between Hosmer and Hillsview puffing up a white plume of steam and whistling at every road crossing. Snowbanks didn't stop the train from making its run to Strasburg, North Dakota. When the train encountered a snowbank, the engineer unhooked the cars and pushed through the snowbank with the snowplow that was connected to the front of the train engine. On its journey north, the train engineer dropped off coal cars, loads of lumber and empty wheat cars. The express car carried empty cream cans, mail and light freight that were unloaded and moved into the depot warehouse. A caboose was the last car on the train. It had a small desk for the conductor and a few seats for passengers.

Listening to the train puff its way north to Hillsview, Joe's mind turned to his sister who frequently met the train walking home from school for lunch. The train stopped at the Hosmer depot around noon. She watched soldiers arrive in Hosmer by train at noon, and later in the day soldiers would leave town on the train heading south to Roscoe and beyond.

On her way home after school, she picked up mail at the post office. She got letters from her girlfriends who had left the farm and got wartime jobs in Minneapolis, Chicago and other big cities on the West Coast. Occasionally, her boyfriend Johnny Hoffman mailed her a note setting up a date for a movie or dance in town. She dated Johnny secretly because Carl didn't want Cathy to hang around Catholic boys. Johnny was Catholic.

Cathy liked staying in town to attend high school because it allowed her to partake in school activities. She was in a school play and tried out as a cheerleader. When she drove the model A Ford car to school, she had to return to the farm to do chores and missed out on extra school activities. Grandma's house didn't have electricity, running water or a sewer. Cathy carried water over from a neighbor's well. She took her bath in a galvanized tub in the living room and did her thing in an outhouse. She begged her mother for a battery-powered radio, but because of the wartime shortage, she had to do without a radio. The farmhouse had indoor plumbing, electricity and a warm bedroom. Cathy reconciled that life had different trade-offs.

The county plowed the road to Hosmer allowing Carl, Gertrude and Joe to drive into town on Saturday evening without chains on the car tires. Joe dreaded the trip to town when a rabbit ran across the road. His dad would stop the car in the middle of the road and turn on his homemade spotlight, shine it on the rabbit, blinding him and then shoot it with his 22-caliber rifle. He made Joe get out of the car, stumble through snow in the ditch and oftentimes he had to squeeze between strands of barbwire fence to retrieve an injured rabbit from a farmer's field. An injured rabbit's distress call is a high-pitched hideous cry. Joe frequently had to finish killing the rabbit by whacking its head on frozen ground to put the rabbit out of its misery. Carrying bleeding rabbits smeared Joe's pants. This distressed Joe tremendously. Carl's nighttime rabbit hunting disturbed Gertrude. She said, "Stop shooting rabbits with the spotlight. It's against the law." She knew her son didn't relish chasing after bleeding rabbits in his good clothes. Joe hunted rabbits on Sunday afternoons in the old Model T truck. Farmers tied the rabbits' hind legs together with twine and hung them on a nail on the north side of the barn to keep them frozen. That winter Joe and Carl had thirty rabbits hanging in two rows on the north side of their barn. Lots of rabbits hanging on the north side of a barn showed macho pride. The hide and junk buyer in town shipped out frozen rabbits in an open freight car to Chicago where they were skinned for their hides and the rest of the rabbit was ground up into cat and dog food.

Their first stop in town was at Grandma Schultz's house. They dropped off milk, cream, eggs, a butchered chicken, a beef roast and some sausage. Grandma didn't eat much herself but Cathy, her boarder, had a good appetite. Carl gave Grandma money for extra expenses incurred on behalf of Cathy. Cathy usually was already uptown by the time Carl, Gertrude and Joe arrived. Joe figured that she was most probably making out with Johnny Hoffman in his car parked in some remote place. Cathy and Johnny liked to take in the weekly movie on Saturday night. Gertrude knew that they were dating on the sly but didn't mention it to Carl. It didn't bother Gertrude as it did Carl that Johnny was Catholic.

Their next stop was the creamery to drop off a crate of 144 eggs and a can of cream. Then Carl sold the rabbits he shot on the way into town. Gertrude went to a grocery store, Carl to the implement dealership and Joe went to the pool hall. After Carl did his buying of new machine parts, welding rods and other odds and ends for the blacksmith shop, he went to the pool hall for a game of cards, drank a few draft beers and chewed some sunflower seeds. Joe wasn't into playing card games; he played pool and pinball machines. At home, Cathy and Joe had to join in with their parents in playing Hearts and other versions of that basic game that required four players. Both Joe and his sister developed a dislike for card games because their father insisted that they play to his expectations. The right way was the only way because that was Carl's way. Family card games at the Schultz farm ended acrimoniously.

After Gertrude finished her shopping, she drifted from the grocery store to the creamery to pick up her cream-and-egg check. This was her last place to socialize with neighbor folks before driving home. Gertrude waited patiently for the two men in her life to show up at the creamery. The only time women stepped into a pool hall was in case of an emergency and then they would wait at the very front of the pool hall for whomever they were looking for. Both pool halls had a bar on one side and booths to the opposite side where men played card games. At the front end of the bar, there were punchboards that cost five, ten or twenty-five cents per punch. Prizes ranged fifty cents to ten dollars. Beef jerky and a large jar of pickled eggs were on the other end of the bar. Pinball machines and pool tables were in the back half of the pool hall. The rear door of the pool hall led to an outhouse across the alley. After a few beers, guys peed against the outhouse and around the coal shed.

Driving home Gertrude calculated in her mind the total egg-and-cream money minus what she spent on groceries that evening. She bought groceries and clothes for the family and also gave Cathy and Joe spending money. Carl kept track of wheat, cattle and hog money. That was the big income on the farm.

* * * * *

In January, a hellish storm blew in as Joe came riding home from school on Sam. They did chores early before darkness set in. They went to bed expecting snowdrifts around every building on the farm and snowbanks across the road by morning. Joe was slow getting out of bed the next morning. He didn't go out to the barn and to feed Sam his oats before the ride to school. He had no intention of going to school in a raging storm. He still had memories of that blinding snowstorm he and Sam had stumbled through. Sam may have forgotten, but Joe would never forget that miserable, scary day.

Carl and Gertrude got up late in semi-darkness. Carl heard the porch door close as he pulled the overhaul straps over his shoulders. He walked barefoot to check the door when he saw through the front window a man walking in swirling snow toward the county road. Apparently, the man had come into the house during the night and slept in front of the kitchen stove. When the stranger heard Carl moving around in the bedroom, he got up and left.

After breakfast there still was no sun in sight, but the darkness of the night had faded. Joe dressed and went outside to do morning chores. He saw a black-and-white dog curled up by the house. He dashed back into the house and told his dad that the mysterious traveler had left a dog behind. Gertrude peeked out of the kitchen window and smiled when she saw the dog. She put chunks of bread and scraps of meat into a bowl. She poured milk over it and handed it to Joe and said, "Go feed the dog." Joe took the bowl of scraps and placed it by the dog and said, "It's okay, go eat it." The dog eyed Joe and then the bowl of food but didn't eat the scraps. Joe went back into the house and watched the dog through the kitchen window. After the dog finished eating, Joe went outside and petted the dog and retrieved the bowl. The dog sniffed Joe and wagged its tail. A lifetime bond was made between dog and man.

Joe was surprised and delighted when his dad said that he welcomed the dog. Joe gleefully dressed in his overcoat, overshoes, gloves, and cap with the earflaps and went about putting hay into feeding racks for the cows in the barn, scooped manure from the cows' stalls and pitched it to the front of the barn and then checked the cattle water tank. It was frozen. The wind had blown out the water heater. Joe was very careful in igniting the excess heating oil. He put a match to a small rag soaked with fuel oil and dropped it down into the puddle of oil. A blast of flames shot up and the heater rocked as fire spewed out of its chimney like a blasting torch. He remembered the time he lit the flooded heater and singed his eyebrows.

The dog followed Joe around wherever he went and watched him intently. That night Carl took the dog into the barn to sleep under Sam's crib. He saw that the dog was a female. Joe and his mother discussed a name for the female dog before going to bed that night. The next morning, Gertrude came up with name Shep because the dog looked like a sheepherder's dog. After breakfast, Joe let Shep out of the barn when he fed Sam his oats. Shep stayed close to the house until Joe rode off to school on Sam. She didn't know if she should follow Joe and Sam or stay at the farm. Gertrude put out table scraps for Shep in hopes that she would eat them and not follow Joe and Sam to school. Shep watched Joe ride away on Sam and spent the rest of day following Carl around the farm.

It didn't take Carl long to nail together a doghouse with old lumber he had stacked next to the garage. He lined the inside of the doghouse with an old sheepskin coat that was brought over from Russia by his grandfather. The floor of the doghouse rested on blocks of wood to keep it off the ground. Carl shoveled snow against the walls to keep wind from blowing under and into the doghouse. A gunnysack hanging over the doghouse door kept snow from blowing in. The doghouse looked like it was buried in a snowbank.

Carl rummaged through a pile of old car parts and found a round cast iron piece that once was the housing of a gearbox and made a chow bowl for the dog. Shep took to her new home with enthusiasm. Without any prodding, she slept in her house that night and thereafter. It remained a mystery where Shep was born or to whom she had belonged at one time. The only thing known about Shep was that she arrived at the farm in a snowstorm with a stranger who slept in Schultz's house for a night and left the next morning without speaking a word to anyone.

* * * * *

March was calving time. Carl and Gertrude went to the neighbors to play cards and left Joe at home to look after a heifer. It was the heifer's first pregnancy, and Gertrude questioned her ability to give birth by herself. Before going to bed, Joe went out to the barn and checked on her. Sure enough, the heifer was lying down with two calf legs sticking out of her rear. He debated pulling the calf out with a wire stretcher. He had watched his dad and mom pull a calf from a heifer one time. He didn't attempt to assist the heifer in birthing because she was lying down and he was alone. Cathy was staying in town with Grandma.

He went into the house, sat down at the kitchen table and rested his head on his arms on the table. He promptly fell asleep. An hour later, he awoke when his parents opened the front door. Joe told them about the heifer. They quickly changed clothes and lifted the heifer to her feet and pulled out the calf. The calf was dead, but they saved the heifer. Gertrude suggested to Carl that the heifer should be sold because she had a small utter and would never be a productive milk cow. Carl motioned his head in agreement.

Spring came and melting snow filled all the ponds, sloughs and lakes with water. It looked promising for a bumper wheat crop this year and a good year for hay. Sprouting green grass emanated a sweet aroma. Cows stopped eating hay and turned to green pastures. The change in their diet gave milk a taste of onions. The onion flavor in the milk and manure smell on Joe's hands from squeezing cow teats destroyed his taste for milk forever. His mother asked him to be patient and that the onion taste would disappear in time. She pointed out to him that milk cows would be spending very little time in the barn and their teats wouldn't be smeared with manure anymore. He was supposed to wash manure off their teats with warm water but neglected to do so and had to suffer smelly hands.

Joe returned to his sunrise routine of finding the horses and then luring Sam to him with a small pouch of oats. After mounting Sam, he drove the horses in the direction of the farm. Shep bit a couple of horses in the hind legs and that made them take off in a gallop toward the farm. Joe went in search of the cattle with Shep in tow. Shep immediately took over and got the slow, lazy cattle into a trot in the direction of the farm. Shep moved behind the cattle from one side to the other not to let any of them stray. Joe and Shep together drove the horses and cattle back to the farm for about a week. At the end of that week, on a Sunday morning, Joe overslept because of a late Saturday night in town. The sun had been above the horizon for about thirty minutes when he awoke. He quickly got dressed and walked past the barn, across the slough and toward the first hill east of the farm when he saw a herd of cattle coming down the hill in a fast trot. Cattle walking on their own volition did so normally at a slow pace. Shep had gone out into the pasture at sunrise and fetched the herd by herself. She did what she had been bred and trained to do. In the evening, milk cows would come back to the farm and wait around the barnyard to be milked. If they weren't at the farm in time for milking, Joe sent Shep after them and went about to do his chores of slopping mash to the hogs, feeding and watering the chickens, collecting eggs and then helped his mother taking harnesses off the workhorses.

In spring, at the beginning of planting, Cathy started driving to high school every day, and this relieved Joe from milking cows. He didn't like milking cows. He thoroughly enjoyed having Cathy around for company. He got lonesome on the farm without her. This particular evening, Joe helped Cathy and his mother milk cows because he had finished doing chores before all the cows were milked. Gertrude, Cathy and Joe carried on a fluid gabfest verifying rumors and making small talk as they finished milking the last cows.

Gertrude became unglued when she saw an emaciated cat and three tiny kittens enter the barn and approach her for milk. Gertrude grunted, "Ach, Mein Gott." Joe and Cathy saw the undernourished cat with her kittens. Gertrude poured fresh, warm milk into a saucer that was kept around the barn for the cats. The mother cat and her three kittens lapped up the milk vigorously. A week previously, Gertrude had placed six kittens into a gunnysack weighted down with a rock and dropped them into a shallow lake one and a half miles from the farm. This was her way of controlling the cat population on the farm. Joe said, "Ma, I told you that I should shoot the females and then we wouldn't have to kill kittens all the time. Dad makes me shoot everything else on this farm." Gertrude was upset over her failure and said to Joe, "Next time you take them up the hill and smash their heads on the rock pile." Apparently, the mother cat found her way to the lake and retrieved three living kittens and moved them with her mouth one by one over the distance of one and a half miles. She had been without water for days and must have fed on mice on her long trip back to the farm.

A month later, Joe trudged up the hill north of the farm and smashed five newly born kittens on a large rock in the rock pile. He hated himself for doing this. It was so cruel. He became more and more distraught every step of the way back to the farm. His dad and mother no longer could stomach killing so they made him do it.

After they finished milking, they ran the milk through a cream separator. Cathy cranked the separator by hand. Joe fed skimmed milk to the calves and Gertrude attended to cooking supper. At sunset, Carl stopped plowing with the tractor and drove home in the Model T truck. This was pretty much how every day ended on the farm during spring.

A typical morning on the Schultz's farm always started the same way from spring planting though thrashing in the fall. Chores were the very first thing done in the morning and the last in the evening. After spring planting, there were fences to fix, haying and rocks to pick off cultivated land. Picking rocks was an endless task. Over the years, rocks would squeeze to the surface from below ground due to expansion and contraction caused by freezing and thawing every year. Joe suggested that his dad build a rock picker. Carl said that they could scoop up large rocks with the front-end loader on a new Farmall tractor. During days of rock picking, Joe's mind wandered. He thought of life on the farm like the endless furrow that he followed while plowing with the tractor. He drove up and down a field plowing all day long and the next day and the next day. Occasionally, a plowshare got caught on a buried rock and the plow disengaged from the tractor hitch. That broke Joe's dazing spell. For a teenager, life on the farm could be an eternal treadmill.

Repetitious life on the farm was not without changes in Cathy and Joe's lives. This was Joe's last year at the country grade school, and this fall he would be a freshman in high school and drive to school with Cathy. In late summer, he would attend confirmation class and be confirmed in the German Reformed Church. Joe switched from memorizing the Heidelberg Catechism in German to English, much to the dismay of his father. He told his mother he wouldn't memorize the catechism in the German. He didn't even like the language. He didn't like the minister at the German Reformed Church because of his Hitler-like mentality. He developed an aversion toward organized religion at a young age. Joe's rebellious tendencies became more and more apparent in his teen years.

Carl was accumulating money from good crops and high WWII prices for grain, hogs and cattle. He wanted to buy a couple of new tractors and replace horsedrawn equipment, but the war prevented farm equipment from being manufactured. His friend, the local farm equipment dealer, promised him a new tractor in the spring. Carl had no idea how the dealer would come up with a new tractor during WWII. Carl didn't ask any questions and kept this matter to himself. The equipment dealer knew that after the war ended, Carl would buy lots of farm machinery from him.

Carl decided to spend money on the house and granary. He had the house movers raise the house and dug out a basement under it. He abandoned the windmill and installed a submerged electric water pump. In this way, he supplied water to the cattle trough and pumped water up to the house. He had a septic hole dug. Indoor plumbing eliminated the need for a two-hole outhouse. In the winter, the outhouse was miserably cold and in summer there was that pungent stench and the flies that loved the place. The coal furnace was replaced with a fuel oil furnace and an oil-fired hot water heater was installed. All these improvements were available from the local lumberyard. New cars and tractors farmers could only dream about until the war was over.

Farmers quit farming for one reason or another despite good times. Some farms were too small and unproductive, and other farmers sold out because they wanted to retire and move to town. Carl had money in savings at the bank and wanted to spend it on improvements and expand the farm. He was looking to buy more land adjacent to his farm. At the supper table, he told the family that he was doing all this for Joe who soon would be taking over the farm. Joe almost choked on his father's comment. Cathy giggled knowing that Joe hated the farm. Joe's dislike for life on the farm was mostly because of his dad's obsession about the farm. Joe had no idea how he was going to escape from the farm, but vowed that he would leave it some day.

Chapter VII

Joe was confirmed and decided to stay away from churches. Before being confirmed, he had to sit at the front of the church for Sunday school classes on the left side of the church. Women sat on the left side and the men on the right side. The German-Russians had their own approach to segregation. After confirmation, he slipped into the last bench in back of the church with other young guys who were forced to attend church occasionally. Shortly after confirmation, he had to sit in front of the church with five other young fellows as pallbearers. Sitting in front of the church brought to mind his experience of sitting up front in an open forum for confirmation.

One of his classmates was so terrified by the minister's question-and-answer session of confirmation that he threw up in front of the entire congregation. He was excused from the class. Weeks later, after much debate, he was confirmed by the minister in a private session. The minister wanted the boy to go through confirmation class a second time the following year. The young man's father insisted that his son be confirmed or he would leave the German Reformed

Church. The despotic minister, concerned with a shrinking congregation, thought better and confirmed the boy.

Joe had a bad start as a freshman in high school. His dad kept him and Cathy out of school to man a bundle wagon to thrash oats and barley. Carl was short one bundle wagon because of the death of his neighbor. He agreed to thrash grain for the dead man's wife. Carl hired his dear friend the German Reformed minister to replace the missing man of his thrashing crew. Joe was thrilled to be confirmed and forever rid of the minister and now he had to spend the entire thrashing season in his company. On the second day of pitching bundles, the minister's hands blistered so badly he had to quit the job. Joe was happy that the minister left the thrashing crew. Joe's sadistic happiness was short-lived. The minister's hands healed and he returned to haul bundles.

Joe missed the start of classes and baseball and basketball practice. At a height of five feet and eight inches, he was too short for basketball and his hands were too small to handle the basketball. He didn't like basketball. He was a good baseball player because his dad had taught him the basics of the game.

Carl and Gertrude picked and husked corn by hand with a team of horses and a wagon. They cut sorghum and corn stalks and then stacked them at the farm. This was hard work in the fall. The payoff was selling cattle and hogs at the Aberdeen sale barn and wheat at the local elevator.

After missing the first three weeks of school, Cathy and Joe drove to school every day in the Model A Ford. Sometimes they stayed overnight at Grandma Schultz's house to participate in a school event. Joe had a surprise when he showed up for his algebra class. The teacher was the German Reformed minister. There was a shortage of manpower, including teachers, due to the war. Joe studied hard and did well in algebra despite his inept teacher because his father had helped him in grade school with arithmetic. Cathy was back to tutoring Joe in his English lessons like she did when they both were in grade school.

In the fall, Carl moved the cattle and horses to harvested fields west of the farm. There was undergrowth in those fields and some grass in dried-out sloughs. Cattle always came back to the farm before sunset for a drink of water and a night's rest in the corral. Horses had an independent way of showing up late at night or not at all. On this day, the horses found an open gate west of the farm and were feeding on grass along the section line road. Carl told Joe to round up the horses and herd them back to the farm before dark. Joe took Sam's bridle and some oats in a paper bag and walked along the fence bordering the section line road to where the horses were grazing. He did his routine with Sam and mounted him by a fence and lashed out at the horses. A feisty mare heaved her hind hoofs up at Sam. Sam turned sideways to avoid the kick, exposing Joe's knee to the mare's hoof. Her kick hit Joe's right knee and knocked him off Sam.

He tore a hole in his overcoat when he fell off Sam into a barb-wired fence. Sam and the other horses took off in a gallop down the road to the farm. He got up, put his cap on and attempted to walk on the road. His knee was in pain and swelling. He couldn't walk on it. He had to drag it along. It started to snow and turned dark quickly. Joe didn't know how long he could manage to drag his foot along the wagon road. He was a half-mile from home.

Gertrude had turned on the yard light by the windmill to watch for Joe's return. She saw Sam galloping with the horses into the corral. Reins were flapping on Sam's side and no rider was his back. Carl removed Sam's bridle and returned to the house. He was puzzled over what might have happened. Joe had never fallen off Sam before. Carl and Gertrude drove along the section line road and found Joe dragging his left leg in the fresh snow. After a miserable night, they took Joe to Wishek, North Dakota, to a chiropractor. His kneecap had been dislodged from the kick by the mare. Two weeks later, Joe hung up his crutches and no longer was a cripple.

In midwinter Shep disappeared one night. Joe checked the doghouse several times hoping she had returned. On the second day, he looked for her around the farm and there was no sign of Shep. He reasoned that Shep had arrived unexpectedly on a stormy night and decided to leave on a beautiful bright moonlit night. On the third morning, he found her sleeping in the doghouse. He spoke to her, "Shep, you are home again." She opened her eyes and then closed them, ignoring him. He noticed blood oozing on her belly in front of her rear left leg. He didn't see any scars indicating a fight with another dog. He looked more closely and concluded that she had been shot, probably with a rifle. She didn't eat anything for two days. Joe thought she was preparing herself to die. The third day she lapped up milk and moved around gingerly. She had lived another day.

On Saturday evening, Carl sauntered into his favorite pool hall and met his neighbor Heinrich who lived to the east of the Schultz farm. Heinrich broached the subject of dogs chasing his cattle on ice on a moonlit night on a frozen pond. He said, "I shot a black-and-white collie. I think she was in heat and that is why all the neighboring dogs got together and chased my heifers on the ice. They had a party. My son and I butchered the heifer that broke her leg on the ice." Carl stared at the floor and changed the subject to a high-low-jack game of cards that was being organized. They sat down in a booth with two other men and played cards. Carl didn't tell his friend Heinrich that his black-and-white female collie had been shot.

Carl turned on the radio for the evening news broadcasts during suppertime to check on how the war was getting along. Hitler, the evil man in Europe, was losing battle after battle. The Japanese were still dug in on islands all over the Pacific Ocean. Soldiers got off the train in town on crutches, and some arrived in pine boxes. WWII was leaving its emotional and physical scars on all Americans, including folks on the prairie.

* * * * *

Joe didn't fare too well in hunting or doing the killing on the farm. Two weeks after he stoned five of a cat's litter, he had the shock of his life. While he, Cathy and their mother were milking one evening, the cat with two kittens, one with a cauliflower ear walked in for some fresh milk. The little angora kitten with the cauliflower ear had survived Joe's attempted execution. The mother cat retrieved it from the rock pile and nursed it to health. The other four kittens he had stoned remained dead. When the cat with her kittens parked in the middle of the barn begging for milk, Joe poured some into a dish and said nothing. He swore that he would find some other way of keeping the cat population in check.

He went rabbit hunting on a moonlit night riding Sam across snowdrifts. Seated on Sam, he fired the rifle at a rabbit in close range. The shot spooked Sam. He leaped forward and Joe did a summersault backwards off Sam into a hard snowbank. He stuck the rifle butt into the snowbank, got back on Sam, pulled up the rifle from the snowbank and rode home. He baited a steel trap with chicken liver to trap a wily weasel that hung around the chicken coop. The next morning he found a dead cat with its neck caught in the trap frozen solid as a rock. He kept that embarrassing mishap to himself.

Never bagging a partridge was one of his most frustrating failures. A covey of partridges lived by a cottonwood tree just across the road from the farm. Many times he took his dad's old single-shot twelve-gauge gun and fired into the flock of partridges and never hit one. The covey of partridges flew repeatedly from their feeding ground to a sheltering spot. They never left their habitat despite Joe firing lead at them. They aggravated and frustrated him for many seasons, and eventually he gave up on them.

* * * * *

Spring came and Shep was pregnant and soon to give birth to pups. Franklin Delano Roosevelt said that the war in Europe would end this spring. America was waiting with great anticipation for that day to come. After three years of wartime, the shortage of many things and men going off to war had become a way of life in America, but life on the prairie remained pretty much the same: young women gave birth to children and old folks died. Carl volunteered Joe as a pallbearer again. He had to attend services at the German Reformed church against his wishes.

Seated in the front bench of the church with five men he had to listen to a hell and damnation sermon by the minister that he despised. His thoughts drifted back to his recent confirmation when the minister laid out his personal edicts. The confirmation class was instructed to never attend a Catholic Church under any circumstances. Flowers were not allowed inside the church, not even for a wedding or a funeral. The German Reformed Bible had to be without religious pictures. Only the word of God was allowed in the German Reformed Bible and church. The minister was a follower of Calvin and Zwingli, two Swiss Protestant reformers who didn't think that Martin Luther went far enough with his Reformation movement. He told the class that should they move away from Hosmer, they were expected to locate in a town that had a German Reformed church. Joe's reminiscing of past experiences in this church made him itchy. He couldn't wait for the funeral to end. Like on previous visits to church, he swore to distance himself from this mad man, the minister.

President Franklin Delano Roosevelt died and the nation mourned. War in Europe ended and Shep gave birth to six puppies. Gertrude gave away five of the puppies and kept one that Cathy selected as her dog. She named him Pup. Life on the prairie was due for rapid changes in farming with new tractors, trucks, cars and modern farm machinery soon available. In some aspects, life had not changed. Gertrude still canned carrots, beets and had a crock full of melons in brine for the winter months. She stored potatoes in gunney sacks on dry ground in the corner of the cellar. Onions and garlic were strung up on a line in the cellar. She still baked bread but bought sliced bread to make ham and cheese sandwiches for lunch out in the field. Carl didn't make his own beer and wine anymore. He bought that in town but continued to make his schnapps. There was no schnapps he liked better than his own concoction.

Planting the land in spring went smoothly. Gertrude worked her team of horses in the field like she had for years. Carl plowed with the old 15/30 International and Joe plowed, drilled and harrowed with the new International M Farmall. Haying was still done with horse-drawn equipment. They made extra hay by cutting grass on section lines and ditches along the country road that bordered their land. Ditches were free of whiskey, wine and beer bottles because Cathy and Joe picked them up along with metal and rubber that they sold to the scrap dealer in town for spending money. The government had encouraged folks to collect and ship metal and old rubber tires back East to be reprocessed into new tires and lots of bombs. Carl loaded all his excess metal from the junk pile and old tires on the truck and hauled it to town during the war. The countryside was as clean as the day settlers arrived in the late 1880s. The throwaway society was a couple of decades in the making.

Harvesting was finally finished at the end of August, and the war with Japan ended after President Harry Truman dropped two atomic bombs on Japan. Threshing became a real problem because Heinrich had bought a threshing machine and the other neighbor had retired and sold his farm to Heinrich. Carl had planned to thresh his harvest and Hoffman's with three bundle wagons. Johnny Hoffman and his dad each hauled bundles with their respective wagons. Cathy and Joe together manned a wagon. The old Case threshing machine worked a normal load with bundles delivered by five or six bundle wagons in the field. Carl had only three bundle wagons feeding the threshing machine and therefore had to shut down the machine and wait for wagons to unload. He could see that his custom threshing days were nearing an end.

Cathy and Joe had a mishap that confirmed Gertrude's worst fears about two young people trying to do a man's job. Their team of two horses took off and tipped over the wagon. A swarm of bees spooked the team. They took off with the wagon, making a sharp turn downhill, tipping over the wagon. The horses came to a stop when the wagon turned over. Johnny Hoffman came to Cathy and Joe's rescue. With his team of horses and the wagon, he pulled the tipped wagon upright. Carl managed to finish threshing his and Hoffman's harvest on time. Cathy and Joe returned to classes in high school. Carl and Gertrude picked corn and readied the farm for winter.

Pup, Cathy's dog, developed a bad habit of chasing cars on the county road and riding on the fender of the Model A Ford. Joe stayed out of school to help corral steers for shipment to the Aberdeen Sales Barn. Cathy made the mistake of letting Pup ride on the fender of her car all the way to school. Pup leaped to the running board of the car and then scooted forward on the fender and wedged himself between the hood and fender of the car. At school Pup stayed by the car briefly and then wandered around town the rest of the day. After school let out, Cathy drove through town looking for Pup and found him at the senior citizens' home. He leaped on the fender, hugging the headlight with his paw and enjoyed the thrill of his life, the ride home.

At suppertime Cathy told the family that Pup went to town with her that day and spent most of it at the senior citizens' home. Her dad said that she should chain up Pup in the morning and not let him ride to town with her. He reminded her that the high school superintendent took issue with him because Pup roamed around town by himself. Cathy explained that Pup visited with folks around town and always ended up at the senior citizens' home. She said, "They look forward to Pup's visit. They save goodies for him." Joe joined in by saying, "Pup is supposed to be a farm dog and not a town pet." Cathy responded quickly to Joe and said, "He is my dog and he is none of your business." The following day, when Cathy turned the car toward the county road, Pup ran along the side of the car and prepared to make the leap to the running board and then onto the fender. Joe, seated in the passenger side of the car, opened the door and kicked Pup in the rear on the run. He tumbled sideways and stayed home that day. The following week Joe stayed home to help finish picking corn. Cathy allowed Pup to ride to town with her. She stopped at Grandma Schultz's house to look after her before driving to school on the other side of town. She had to decide whether to lock Pup up in the car all day or leave him at Grandma Schultz's place. She opted to leave Pup in Grandma's outhouse. After school, she let Pup out of the outhouse and watched him run around in circles a few times showing his happiness to see Cathy and being let out of jail. He leaped on the fender of the Model A and snuggled himself between the radiator and headlight on the fender of the car for the ride home. Cathy didn't linger much at Grandma's house because heavy winter weather was moving in from the north.

She started the car and slowly drove in a snowfall out of town north toward the farm. Snow from the previous night had melted during the day and was rapidly freezing. She drove erratically over icy spots, oversteering the car. One mile from the farm she crossed a very icy stretch of road that went through a slough. The rear end of the car started to slide sideways. She overcorrected steering the car and did a complete 360-degree turn. The car slid into the ditch and turned over twice, rolling up against the burrow. She was numb and disoriented from the crash. She crawled out of the car and started to walk home. Ahead on the crest of the hill she saw Pup running full tilt. She assumed that he must have leaped off the car fender as it tumbled into the ditch and bolted from the wreck in a hurry.

Gertrude was walking up from the barn and saw Pup lying by his little house panting. She immediately concluded that something bad had happened on Cathy's drive home from school. She drove the Plymouth down the road toward town. On the crest of the first hill south of the farm, she saw Cathy on foot and the Model A in the ditch. Cathy hysterically reiterated what had happened as she drove across the icy road. Gertrude got out of her car and examined the damage. She switched off the idling engine. In a daze, Cathy had left the engine running. Carl and Gertrude righted the car with the tractor and pulled it out of the ditch. Miraculously, there was no mechanical damage, only a few scratches and dents on the body of the car.

Family events of the day were discussed at the supper table. On this evening, the subject was Cathy's car crash. Joe abruptly concluded that the accident happened because Cathy was distracted by Pup riding on the fender of the car. Cathy vigorously denied that Pup was the cause of the accident. Joe empathically said, "I am going to shoot that worthless dog." His comment started a hot debate between brother and sister. Carl smirked over the siblings' argument. He was in agreement with Joe but chose not to meddle. Carl explained to Joe how he could wire the car with a coil and shock Pup as he hit the running board of the car. Cathy cringed at the thought of torturing her pet and hastily left the supper table in dismay.

The next morning, Cathy drove the car to the county road with Joe in the passenger seat. When Pup made a mad leap for the running board, Joe opened the car door and kicked him in the butt. Pup tumbled over sideways and missed his ride that day. Pup always rode on the passenger side of the car. He never rode on the driver's side of the car.

Joe mounted an old coil on the firewall of the Model A and wired it to the car battery. After Joe finished installing a switch, he said to his dad, "I wonder if it really works." Carl seated himself in the driver's seat and told Joe to touch the car. He flipped on the toggle switch, and Joe jumped backwards and exclaimed, "Holy smoke, that was one hell-of-a jolt. This should teach Pup a shocking lesson or two." After Joe shocked Pup a few times, the dog soon figured out how to get on the fender and avoid being shocked. Pup jumped right up on the fender and avoided grounding himself from the running board. The dog was determined to fulfill his selfish pleasures. Pup never learned anything meaningful from his mother, Shep. The only thing he inherited from his mother was his physical makeup. Joe didn't stop tormenting Pup and was adamant that he would teach the dog obedience. He started the Model A and sat in it, idling the engine. He tempted Pup to climb up to the fender, but Pup didn't take the bait. The dog waited for the car to start moving before leaping up on the fender. Joe knew that sooner or later Pup would take a pee against one of the wheels. Dogs like to pee over other dogs' scents on auto wheels. Joe sadistically turned on the juice to the coil and shocked Pup though his stream of pee that went from his penis and down to his legs that grounded the charge. Pup jumped up in the air yipping. He went and laid down by the doghouse and sulked mournfully.

Joe persuaded Cathy that he drive the car to school. He drove slowly out to the county road, letting Pup chase the car. He steered the car to the right shoulder of the road and spun the rear wheels spraying Pup with loose gravel. The dog stumbled into the ditch and stopped his chase. Cathy said, "Sometimes I think you are as mean as dad." Joe chuckled and gleefully smiled. He won a battle with Pup on this day but the war was yet to be fought. He enjoyed his revenge of the moment.

Chapter VIII

The war was over and servicemen were being discharged by the droves. Nearly every day more GIs came home by train. The two older Hoffman brothers had fought from Africa up through Italy and on into Berlin without a scratch. The younger Hoffman brothers, who had been assigned to the Pacific theater, didn't fare so well. One returned on crutches with a shattered knee and the other one came home in a pine box. Big changes were about to take place on the prairies at the end of WWII.

Farm boys left for the service as young, naïve county bumpkins and returned as mature young men who had seen more of the world than McPherson County, their birthplace. Some settled down in town and others went back to their roots, the family farm, and many left for life in a big city that they had become acquainted with during the war. There were ample non-farm opportunities in big cities because the country was preparing to satisfy pent-up demand from the Depression and war days. The two older Hoffman brothers each bought a farm adjacent to their dad's farm. The Hoffman boys became some of the first corporate farmers on the prairies. They bought big equipment and farmed each other's acreages in an efficient manner.

One former serviceman in town decided to build a combination movie house and dance hall. Cathy was all excited about the new dance hall. Her dancing was limited to a few high school dances and an occasional barn dance. Barn dances were held in an empty hayloft. Milo was spread on the rough floor to make it slide like a waxed dance floor. Cathy and Joe had seen their first movie before the end of the war. In reality, it was a drive-in movie, a precursor to an in-house theater. A businessman in town had bought a projector, rented a black-and-white western film and showed it on white bedsheets nailed against the white wall of the lumberyard for a screen. Folks sat on top of their cars and roofs around the lumberyard building to watch their first movie ever.

The biggest change in life after the war was the absence of rationing. Sugar, shoes, gasoline, tires, new cars and tractors were becoming available to those who had the means to purchase them. Money was no object for Carl Schultz and other hard- working farmers who had scraped and improvised through the war and saved money. Carl bought another tractor, combine and haying equipment that attached to the tractor.

Gertrude stopped milking cows and let them raise their calves by themselves. She bought her dairy products in town. Cathy and Joe were delighted with her decision. Evening and morning chores were reduced in half from what they used to be. Harvesting with a swather and threshing with a combine, hauling grain with a one-ton dump truck to an elevator in town or storage bin on the farm eliminated the need for horses. Carl sold all his horses accept Sam and a teammate. Sam had been a special horse on the Schultz farm, especially to Joe.

Joe ran the swather, Carl combined and Cathy hauled grain to town or to the grain bins on the farm. This was all done without the use of a single shovel or fork. Manual labor was reduced to operating tractors and trucks.

Farming with tractors rather than horses was a giant leap in the agricultural revolution. A tractor used gasoline only when the engine was running, and at the end of the day it was switched off until the next morning. Horses, on the other hand, ate hay and grain year-round and were a very clumsy source of power on the farm.

During Christmas vacation, Carl and Gertrude decided that Grandma shouldn't live alone in town. They shut down her house and brought her out to the farm. There wasn't much to close down in a house that had no running water or electricity. Grandma was excited to take up residence on the farm. She sat by the window facing the farmyard and watched the Schultz family go about their daily chores. She only saw distant images because she was nearly blind. Cathy had noticed that and mentioned it to her mother. Gertrude had said, "I know that cataracts are clouding her vision."

Grandma was relieved of cooking, doing laundry by hand and didn't have to struggle stoking the coal furnace and hauling coal up stairs to the kitchen stove. She had returned to her real home, the farm. After her husband suddenly died of a massive heart attack, she lost all desire to live in town by herself. Grandma would never return to her house in town again.

After Christmas vacation, Cathy and Joe drove to school every morning and returned in the evening. In the event a storm brewed up, they stayed in town at the piano teacher's house. The piano teacher was a close friend of Gertrude. During the war, Gertrude supplied her with eggs and cream every Saturday night. Cathy and Joe were pleased with this new living arrangement in town. They never liked living at Grandma's house in town because it lacked modern conveniences.

Snowstorms in January frequently spelled disaster for folks on the prairie. In the middle of a three-day cold, windy snowstorm, Grandma Schultz died. Carl was devastated. Gertrude took Grandma's death as a blessing. She sensed that Grandma wanted to die on the Schultz farm and not in her house in town. Gertrude said to Carl, "She came home to die."

Carl and Gertrude put Grandma into her black Russian coat she inherited from her mother and wrapped her with a heavy wool blanket and bedded her down on the front porch. It was below freezing on the porch and that would keep Grandma frozen until the road to town was plowed open. The phone line extended to Hillsview but not beyond anywhere else. Carl called the depot agent in Hillsview and had him telegraph the minister in Hosmer and asked him to make preparations for a funeral. The minister told Cathy and Joe, who were staying in town because of the storm, that Grandma Schultz had died but delayed plans for a funeral until the ground thawed out in early spring.

The road was plowed two miles north of Hosmer to a nine-foot snowbank. It would require a rotator snowplow to dig through the deep, hard windblown snowbank. It was agreed that Carl would bring his mother to the large snowbank and link up with the undertaker. Carl took the farm sledge, put metal runners on it and placed a border around the top to hold Grandma in place for the trip. The next morning he put a light harness on Sam, hitched him to the sled and parked in front of the house. Gertrude placed Grandma's Sunday dress inside the coat she was wrapped in. Carl picked up his petite mother and carefully placed her on the sled. He took a horse blanket and spread it over her. Without another word spoken, he mounted Sam and rode down the county road with Grandma in tow on the makeshift sled. Sam was a big horse; he pulled the sled with ease. He managed to stomp through the first snowbank that was five feet deep on the west side of the road and dropped to a depth of three feet on the other side of the road. The three-foot snowdrift was so hard windblown that Sam didn't even break through it as he walked across it. Runners on the sled made an eerie screeching noise as Sam pulled it across the hard-packed snow. On top of the first hill there was no snow, just gravel. The runners bounced across the gravel as Sam jerked the sled with every large step he took. At the bottom of the hill, it was tough-going. Snow was three feet deep all across this stretch of the road that crossed the slough. Sam huffed and puffed until they reached the other side of the slough and made it to higher ground. Looking ahead, Carl saw a steep snowbank at the entrance of a farm that he and Sam had to cross one way or another. Approaching the snowbank, Carl steered Sam to the eastern edge of the road. The snowbank sloped from the western edge of the road to the east side. The sled went sideways down the embankment and tipped over, spilling Grandma down into the ditch. Carl let Sam cross the snowbank, dragging the sled upside down and then stopped him. He righted the sled, waded through waist-deep loose snow in the ditch and retrieved Grandma. Grandma made a thump when he laid her back on the sled. She was frozen solid. Tears froze to Carl's eyelids as he grabbed Sam's hame on the collar of the harness and heisted himself up on Sam. He signaled Sam into motion with a nudge of his legs to Sam's sides. Carl's mind drifted from his dad to his mother in the sled. His dad had died many years ago at a young age from a massive heart attack, and now he was sledding his frozen mother to her grave. She died out of desire. She didn't want to live anymore. Carl whispered, "God, what price she paid for her final peace. I am going to miss you, Mother." Sam raised his head and pointed his ears as if he understood. Carl's mind kept wandering as he and Sam made their way toward their destination, the big snowbank. He reflected on the death of his two younger sisters who are buried in little graves under a cottonwood tree on the farm. One was stillborn and the other died a week after birth. He and his sister Ruth survived the harsh life on the prairie. It flashed though his mind that he had not telegraphed his sister Ruth about their mother's death. He suspected that the minister would tend to that. His mind kept floating about as Sam trudged through snowdrifts. Sam turned his head to a familiar sound, the whistle of the train chugging its way from Hosmer up to Hillsview. Carl saw the plume of steam on the horizon. They arrived at a mammoth-sized snowbank. He could hear a car engine idling and voices a distance down the road. He assumed that the undertaker and his helper were shoveling a path for the hearse. Carl was correct in his assumption. Wheels on the hearse were double-chained and packed with snow from grinding through snowdrifts. There was snow on the running boards and against the radiator from bucking through deep snow. Carl carried Grandma across the snowbank and handed her over to the undertaker and his helper. As they laid her in the hearse, the helper said, "Boy, she is a real stiff." Carl was rightfully offended by the nincompoop's remark but kept his thoughts to himself. The undertaker suggested to Carl that they should store her in the "blue room" until the ground thawed. The blue room was an addition on the north side of the mortuary used specifically to store bodies in caskets through winter until spring. Carl was anxious to have her buried as soon as possible.

Carl made the lonesome ride on Sam back to the farm. Sam followed the path he had made through the snow earlier that morning. He seemed anxious in his stride and probably had his mind on oats and a drink of water. He had chewed on a few clumps of snow, but that only wet his tongue and didn't quench his thirst. Shep ran out to meet Carl and Sam at the road. Pup joined Shep, dancing in a circle, jumping around and barking like the pet dog that he was. The county rotator snowplow chewed a path through the deep snowbank, and the road to Hosmer was open again for travel. Joe and Cathy drove to school the rest of the winter as road conditions permitted. Spring came and the ground thawed.

Paul, Jack and Ruth McGregor came for Grandma Schultz's funeral. Ruth had two arrangements of flowers she had bought in Bowdle and placed them next to Grandma's casket. The minister walked over to Ruth and whispered, "I don't allow flowers in this church. We don't want anything to distract from the word of God." He unceremoniously took the flowers and set them on the porch outside the church.

After Grandma was lowered into her final resting place next to her husband Jacob Schultz, Ruth said to Carl, "Her land, house and all personal belongings are yours. I don't want anything. You folks looked after her all these years."

Carl said, "I don't know if that is right." Jack said he wanted Grandpa's antique pocket watch. Carl said, "You can have it." Then Ruth spoke her final words on the matter, "Now that's all settled." As they left the grave, Gertrude said, "I am happy for Catherine. Now she doesn't have to come to Jacob's grave every Sunday after church. She will lay next to him forever." Gertrude apologized to Ruth for the minister's rudeness and asked the McGregors to stay at the farm for the night. Against Gertrude's wishes, Ruth had accepted an invitation from an old school friend to stay there for the night. Early the next morning, the McGregors headed west across the Missouri River to their ranch.

* * * * *

Carl hired the local auctioneer to sell Grandma's household goods and the house. Gertrude and Cathy selected a few of Grandma's things for keepsakes and inventoried everything else for the auctioneer and then gave the house a good cleaning. Carl and Joe tidied up the yard, chicken coop, barn, fence and gates. Joe remembered that she had buried money near her well. He poked into the ground around the well and found a rusty syrup can full of coins. He washed the silver dollars, fifty-cent pieces, quarters and dimes that amounted to a stash of $75.60. Cathy knew that Grandma hid money around the house. Carl had told her that she did this after the bank stole her $10,000 savings on FDR's bank holiday back in the early 1930s. Cathy found dollar bills in a ceramic cookie jar in the pantry. Gertrude found money stuffed in with Grandpa Schultz's clothes in a chest up in the attic. They were not too surprised to find five- and ten-dollar bills tucked into mattresses and pillows. She had sewn money into her bedspread and slipped money behind framed pictures that hung on the walls. Cathy and Gertrude found a total of $210 hidden in various places. They knew some money was probably missed that was hidden in strange places.

Carl knew that Mr. and Mrs. Hoffman planned on moving to town since their sons had taken over the farm. He was pleased that Mr. Hoffman was the high bidder for Grandma's house. After a long, emotional day, Carl drove the family home to the farm.

On the trip back, Cathy and Joe carried on their personal brother-sister conversation in the back seat of the car. Joe said to Cathy, "I won't miss that house. Never liked that house. No plumbing and that freezing cold bedroom. Won't miss that stinky cold outhouse either." Cathy said, "I won't miss those sponge baths I took in a galvanized bath tub in the middle of the living room." Joe added, "The only reason I kept trying to make the basketball team was because I got to shower after practice at school." "Where is the shower at school? I never saw a shower." "It is next to the furnace under the grade school. There is an underground tunnel from the gym to the grade school furnace room. We had to wear shoes going through the tunnel because of the coal dust and soot on the concrete floor. The guys on the team showered first and used up all the hot water. I seldom got to take a hot shower. Town guys went home to shower. Farm guys didn't have a shower at home so they showered at school." Cathy asked, "Why did you quit basketball?" "Dad didn't let me practice enough to make the team. The coach told dad that I would never make the team unless I attended all the practice sessions." "I had the same problems with school plays and cheerleading practice." "I never liked basketball. I hate the game, too short, hands too small, didn't dribble well, never hit the rim."

Gertrude saw that Carl was driving a wedge between himself and his son. He made him work too much on the farm and didn't allow Joe to enjoy a boyhood life. There was little opportunity for Joe to enjoy his school chums. Carl insisted that the farm came first and then maybe there would be time for play and fooling around. Out of sympathy, Gertrude gave Joe money for piano lessons. He took a few lessons, got bored and gave up on music but kept accepting money for piano lessons from his mother. Joe loved to play pool and that is where the piano lesson money was spent. Gertrude asked her friend the piano teacher how Joe was doing with his lessons, and she told Gertrude that he had stopped taking lessons sometime ago. Gertrude reprimanded Joe for being deceitful.

Joe liked baseball because the ball fit better into his hands. His dad played catch with him but didn't let him practice with the school team. Plowing after school let out was more important than baseball. Grandma once told Joe that Carl was a good baseball player. She said that he was good enough to play in the big leagues. Joe asked, "How did Dad become such a good player?" She explained that his team played every Sunday through the summer months and practiced once or twice during the week after work. Joe gradually learned to dislike what Grandma loved the most, his dad and the farm.

Chapter IX

The end of WWII didn't produce the manpower of pre-war days that Carl anticipated. Those, like the Hoffman brothers, who returned to farming did it in a big way with large, powerful equipment and little manpower. Others went to school on the WWII GI Bill of Rights to become engineers, lawyers, doctors and businessmen. Others took advantage of the "52-20" program. They received $20 every week for fifty-two weeks after their discharge from the service in the form of unemployment compensation or relocation payments. Those fellows lived with their parents and gloated over their heroic past, considering themselves WWII veterans deserving of such largesse. Most veterans, after having been discharged from the service, wore their uniforms with battle ribbons and Combat Infantry Badges proudly and then shed their uniforms and went about establishing themselves in a new life.

In the winter of 1945-46, the days of war rationing were gone. There were no more blackouts of lights at night, and no more black market sales of cream and eggs by Gertrude. Cathy didn't sneak around to buy rare, precious silk stockings from Johnny Hoffman's sister in Minneapolis. Gertrude said,

"The war was hard on everybody, a bit more on some than others. We were lucky Dad and Joe didn't have to serve." She went on to retell the story about a young lady in Hosmer who got married to a chief petty officer in the Navy last year. After the couple bought a marriage license at the Edmunds County Court House in Ipswich, the county clerk gave them her best wishes. The petty officer thanked her and said, "We don't have enough gas ration stamps to drive to Minnesota for our honeymoon." As he and his bride turned to leave, the clerk said, "Wait a minute." The clerk left her office. The two sat down in chairs by the wall and held hands to comfort each other. She started to cry. This was the most important time of her life. The clerk returned with a handful of gas ration stamps she had collected from other employees in the courthouse. She handed the stamps to the petty officer. The bride rose, hugged the clerk and tears of despair turned to tears of joy. After their honeymoon, the petty officer returned to his battleship docked in San Diego and continued to fight the Japanese in the Pacific Ocean. Gertrude said, "You know I saw the Petty Officer in town last week. He told me that they were moving to Denver, Colorado."

* * * * *

Carl was cashing in war bonds and buying new tires and more farm equipment including another tractor. At the supper table, he asked the family in general, "What do you think, should I buy Bill's farm? He is going to quit farming." Joe, in a flippant way, responded, "I don't know and don't care." Carl, in disgust with his son's reply, declared, "We are doing this for you. Someday all this will be yours."

The month of January passed without any major catastrophes. Carl bought Bill's small farm for additional pastureland to raise more cattle. He dismantled the old barns and sheds and used the lumber to build wind brakes and shelter for cattle in the winter months. The Hoffman boys bought the little house and moved it to their farm. Carl decided to simplify his operations to wheat and cattle. He even gave up on hogs. He suggested that Gertrude give up her chickens. She ignored him.

Cathy and Joe drove to school in the Model A Ford every day and then drove back to town to cheer on their basketball team or to attend other school activities. The two siblings were enjoying their last year together. Next fall, Cathy planned to enroll at Northern State Teachers College in Aberdeen, leaving Joe alone on the farm.

* * * * *

Spring came, the grass turned green and rabbits reproduced like rabbits do. Little bunnies abounded on the farmland. Gophers came out of hibernation. Meadowlarks sang their melodious songs. Red-winged blackbirds and cowbirds were everywhere. Swallows were building their mud nests on rafters in the barn. Cattle abandoned the hayrack in the corral and took to munching on green grass. Sam aged rapidly since winter. He looked hollow, bony and ill-kept. Joe thought it was old age. Carl opened Sam's mouth and showed Joe the problem. His teeth were rotting and falling out. Sam was starving to death. He no longer could chew ground oats or anything else. Carl said to Joe, "We have to do what is right for Sam. You go dig a grave on the north side of that rock pile up there." He was pointing north of the barn to a small rock pile by the fence. Joe turned numb. He looked his dad straight in the eye and said, "You do it." Carl raised his voice and emphatically said, "I am telling you to do it. There are no ifs, ands or buts. You do it, I am telling you for the last time." It irked Joe that he had never won a confrontation with his dad and he knew better than to disobey him this time. Carl made him do the killing around the farm, and that was beginning to really gnaw on him. Carl made him shoot hogs and steers for slaughter; Gertrude made him kill kittens. He couldn't bring himself to kill Sam.

It had never crossed Joe's mind that Sam would not live forever. He grew up with Sam, and Sam grew old at the same time. Sam and the boy, a young man now, had so many experiences together it was hard for Joe to comprehend the task of shooting and burying Sam. He understood that it was a necessary mercy killing; nevertheless, he couldn't bring himself to shoot his faithful friend. He talked to Cathy about life with Sam that evening from his bedroom into the wee hours of the early morning. She talked about the many times they shared rides to school on Sam. Cathy was more involved with her dog Pup than Sam. To her Sam, was a good horse and Pup was her personal pet. He stopped talking to her when he heard her snoring in a deep sleep. The next morning, after breakfast without conversation, he went about the horrifying task that lay before him.

With pick and shovel on his shoulders, he shuffled his feet slowly along to the north side of the rock pile, Sam's gravesite. He dug through topsoil easily, but it became difficult as he reached clay and rocks. He had eyeballed the width, length and depth of the grave for Sam. After digging down about halfway, he sat on the west edge of the grave and took a break. He looked up and saw the gopher colony where Cathy had snared gophers, cut off their tails and let them return to their burrows alive. When he finished digging the grave, he leaned the shovel against the rock pile and looked across Sam's grave to the west realizing what he had to do next and whispered to himself, "God, I do hate this place."

He shouldered the pick and returned to the barn. He offered Sam some ground oats, but he refused. He walked Sam over to the watering tank for a last drink of cool water. Sam didn't take a drink. Joe got the feeling that Sam wanted to die, and he had to help him with that today. He grabbed the rickety old shotgun from the harness room and led Sam by his halter around the barn, down the slope, across the slough and up the incline to the freshly dug grave. It was a short distance, but to Joe it was one of the longest trips in his life, barring the ride on Sam in that blinding snow blizzard a few years ago.

He positioned Sam parallel to the grave, took off Sam's halter and stroked his forehead with his right hand. He wanted Sam to leave this world a free horse, no halter and no bridle. He picked up the old single shotgun and positioned himself six feet in front of Sam and took aim. He couldn't pull the trigger. Sam put his head down and snorted. Joe took that as a goodbye and please put me out of my misery. Sam raised his head and looked right at Joe. Joe raised the gun, took aim on the white diamond between Sam's eyes and pulled the trigger. Sam buckled at the knees. Joe dropped the gun and pushed Sam sideways into the grave. Joe glanced toward the farm and saw his dad watching from the corner of the house. For the first time, he saw his father as a macho coward. He whispered to himself, "The bastard." He could see that the grave was slightly too small, but there was not much he could do at this point of the burial except tuck Sam into the grave. He pushed Sam's tail down, moved his hind legs up against the belly. He went to the front end of the grave and pushed Sam's head down in a bend. He forced the right front leg down into the grave. The left leg was stiff and he couldn't bend it. He dug around the leg, haphazardly burying it then feverishly shoveled dirt over Sam. The excess dirt made for a mound over Sam with the hoof of the left leg partially exposed. He took a large rock and placed it on the south end of the grave for a headstone. He put the gun on his right shoulder, the shovel on his left shoulder and walked back to the barn. He was so physically and emotionally drained, he nearly hyperventilated. The blue Dakota sky turned a blur as tears streamed down his cheeks. He hung up the shovel in the harness room and threw the gun with spent shell in the chamber into the corner of the harness room, breaking the gun's stock. That was the last time the old gun would ever be fired. Joe never liked the damn gun. It always kicked him in the shoulder fiercely when he fired at the covey of partridge that lived next to the cottonwood tree by the county road. He never killed a partridge with the old shotgun. On this day, the gun that killed Sam also died a violent death at the hand of Joe.

That evening during supper, Carl outlined the future of the Schultz farm as he envisioned it. No one was interested in his monologue, least of all Joe, who was groping with his dreadful morning experience. Gertrude and Cathy, in sympathy with Joe, limited their verbal expressions to grunts denoting neither agreement nor disagreement with Carl.

* * * * *

Fall came and Joe was left alone with his parents and Pup, the worthless dog. Cathy was attending school at Northern State Teachers College in Aberdeen, Sam was gone and Shep disappeared. Joe asked his mother what could have become of

Shep. He said to his mother, " She never wandered from the farm after her almost fatal romance on ice under a full moon on a winter night a few years ago." Shep's duties had been reduced to guarding open gates in the farmyard. She kept cattle from escaping through open gates. When Gertrude stopped milking cows, Joe had to retrain Shep not to fetch cattle every morning at sunrise. He tied her up at night and released her in the morning. Three times she took off to open pasture in pursuit of the cattle. Joe had to talk her out of it. She was a smart dog and soon grasped the idea that she shouldn't roundup cattle in the pasture every morning and drive them back to the farm. Gertrude explained to Joe that Shep was getting old and went off by herself to die. She said, "Shep stopped eating and her coat isn't shiny anymore. She laid around the doghouse and slept all the time. I think she dug a hole by a rock pile, crawled into it and died. Dogs do that."

Joe felt like his life was fading into the sunset on the Schultz farm. Last spring he had to shoot Sam. This fall Cathy left home for college in Aberdeen. Shep left to die someplace by herself. He wished that he too could pack up and leave, but where would he go. He couldn't support himself living away from home. He was only sixteen years old. He felt in bondage to his father and the farm.

Chapter X

Gertrude pleadingly said to Carl, "We have to do something special for Joe. He has had a bad year. He is very unhappy right now. This spring you made him shoot Sam. This fall Cathy left home for college and Shep went off to die." Carl leaned his chair back against the kitchen wall and said, "Yeah, he has had a tough year. His cousin Black Jack is always asking him to spend some time at the ranch. I think there is a rodeo in Mobridge next weekend. Let's put him on the train in Roscoe and the McGregors can pick him up at the train station in Mobridge." Gertrude didn't hesitate, "Let's do it. I am afraid we are losing him."

Joe was excited at the opportunity to get away from the farm and see his cousin ride broncos in a real rodeo. He thought that his cousin Black Jack lived an exciting life, according to Grandma Schultz. She had told Joe that Jack McGregor was a wild cowboy who drank too much whiskey, chased no-good women, smoked those cigarettes and gambled away his money. Grandma's comments about her grandson intrigued Joe. Black Jack was five years Joe's senior and had lived a wild life like Grandma had said.

Black Jack met Joe at the train station and they headed straight out to the ranch. The trip was exciting from the very start. Jack drove the Cadillac like a racecar out on the open gravel road. They reached a few buildings beside the road that Jack called "Our Indian Town." It was a post office, combination gas station and general store all in one. Jack bought two cases of beer, two bottles of Black Label Jack Daniels and two bottles of Scotch for his dad and then picked up the mail and they were off again, spraying gravel as Jack gunned the Cadillac.

Joe became self-conscious wearing farmer clothes in ranch country. West of the Missouri River everybody wore cowboy hats, cowboy boots, Levi pants, cowboy belts and greeted each other with a howdy and a tip of the hat. Joe's tan pants, loafers and white shirt were the external signs of a Great Plains farmer. His heavy German accent was a dead giveaway that he wasn't aware of because back home everybody had a German accent.

Jack ripped along the gravel road at high speeds, leaving a rooster tail behind. He turned off the state road to two paths that looked like a wagon trail. They crossed a cattle guard that parted a fence line stretching both ways as far as the eye could see. Jack blasted through rock and gravel bottom gullies kicking up dust. He said, "We're on the ranch now. Reach back and grab a couple of beers." Jack held on to the beer and steering wheel with his left hand and took out a Camel cigarette with his right hand. He put the cigarette between his lips and lit it with the lighter in the dashboard. He pressed in the cigarette lighter again, took out another cigarette and said to Joe, "You're old enough to smoke." Joe couldn't refuse his cousin, Black Jack the cowboy. He tried to fake smoking. After a few puffs and a couple of coughs, he gave up on the cigarette and finished off his beer. Joe knew how to drink beer; he was raised on homemade beer.

On their arrival at the ranch, Joe received a western welcome from his aunt and uncle, Ruth and Paul McGregor. Joe made an inspection walk of the ranch to find a few buildings and a vast panoramic view of pastureland and blue sky. When he returned to the house, he said, "Only a few buildings for a big ranch." Jack explained to Joe that a ranch didn't need a lot of buildings. A ranch was pastureland, cattle, a few quarter horses and streams running through hay meadows. Joe saw haying equipment, two tractors, a pickup truck and an army jeep. Joe asked Jack, "Where are the haystacks?" Jack said, "We have haystacks around meadows. In the winter, cattle find shelter in ravines and come out to feed when we put out hay for them."

At dawn, Joe woke to unbelievable stillness. He didn't hear a rooster crow. They didn't have any chickens. There were no hogs, no dairy cows, they didn't even have a dog. The only animals Joe saw were four riding horses in a corral. The hundred and seventy-five head of cattle were nowhere to be seen. Jack had said that they weren't too sure how many head of cattle they had. Indians helped themselves to a steer when they were hungry for beef.

That evening, Mrs. McGregor served baked potatoes, corn, steak and black coffee, with apple pie for desert. At breakfast, they had small beefsteaks, hash browns, two eggs, toast and coffee. They skipped lunch that day and maybe did so on many other days. Joe couldn't comprehend the McGregors' impromptu lifestyle. He did conclude that ranchers ate more steak than anyone else in the country. They ate beef for breakfast, dinner and lunch, if they ate lunch at all. Joe grew up on the Schultz farm eating pork, chicken and lots of sausage, with beef as a special treat. During harvesting time they sometimes ate five times a day.

On Saturday morning, Black Jack and Joe put their suitcases in the back seat. Jack slung his saddle into the trunk with cinch, boots and spurs, leather gloves and his lucky black cowboy hat. Joe asked about the rattlers on each side of his rodeo hat. Jack said, "The sound of a rattler drives broncos crazy. That's my idea anyway. One rattler I cut off a rattlesnake that I killed in the tack room and the other one my mare killed. She hates rattlesnakes. She will rear up and stomp down with her front hoofs and chop them to death. She probably has killed more rattlesnakes than I have."

They got into the Cadillac and ripped across the ranch road, bouncing over bumps and hitting rock bottom into dips. Jack said to Joe, "I have a treat lined up for you. Have you ever been laid?" Joe cleared his throat and confessed,

"No." Jack continued, " I have Kitty, a friend of mine who works as a waitress at the hotel, lined up for you. Kitty and Billy Black Bird are best of friends. Billy and I are getting married come Thanksgiving." Joe was bewildered. He had never met or heard of Kitty or Billy Black Bird before. Billy Black Bird sounded like an Indian name to him. Jack lit a cigarette, looked over to Joe and said, "Let me tell you, we are going to have one helluva time this weekend. Glad you finally made it to the ranch. Wish you could stay longer." Jack turned onto the gravel road and pushed the gas pedal down, spinning the rear wheels. He said, "I once rode in the same rodeo with Casey Tibbs. He is about the best bronco rider I have ever seen ride." Joe tried to absorb Jack's cowboy lingo the best he could. He had never heard of Casey Tibbs; he had never been to a rodeo. Jack kept on talking, "Wait until you meet Billy Black Bird, she is a beauty. She got her teaching certificate after two years at Spearfish. She teaches high school in Mobridge. She is quite a gal."

They arrived in Mobridge shortly before the parade started. Jack told Joe that he would ride in the parade. "Have to go to the other end of town where the parade is gathering. See you at the hotel after the parade." The parade was different than anything Joe had ever seen before. Sioux Indians wearing war bonnets, feathers, beaded vests and carrying ceremonial spears danced around to the beat of their drums. They were full-blooded Sioux Indians dressed in original authentic attire. A small group of Indian women pulled a travois behind a chief and some warriors. Black Jack and other cowboys rode on quarter horses in the parade. Ranchers drove their teams hitched to different types of wagons, a chuck wagon, covered wagon and a hayrack with a cowboy band seated on bales of hay.

After the parade, a rancher unloaded a cow from a trailer at the end of the main street and shot it in the head. This was a treat for the Indians. They gathered around the cow, skinned and butchered it very efficiently. They ate the meat raw. Sioux Indians had been forced to live on a reservation for decades in hopes that they would adopt the white man's way of living. They still preferred their native ways.

Billy Black Bird and her mother, Lady Bird, met Black Jack and Joe at the hotel bar and restaurant. When the two women entered the bar, Jack got off the bar stool and greeted them. Joe's mouth fell wide open as he stared at a beautiful woman and her Indian mother. Billy didn't look like a full-blooded Sioux. Her mother looked like an Indian woman, but Billy didn't look Indian at all. The two gals went to use the bathroom and Jack found a booth for them to sit in. Joe said to Jack, "Boy, she is one good-looking Indian. Ah…. I mean they are two good-looking women." Jack explained Billy's family tree, "Grandma was married to a Frenchmen and Billy's mother got pregnant by an English drifter who didn't stick around to see Billy grow up." Billy's hair was jet black, she had shinny black eyes and an olive complexion. She was a neatly stacked gal in tight jeans, rodeo shirt and a cowgirl hat. She looked like a model and talked like a college girl.

Lady Bird ordered a Coca-Cola; it was illegal for Indians to drink liquor. Billy and Joe both drank beer illegally. Billy was part Indian and Joe was underage. Had Joe's age been questioned, Jack would have vouched for him. Joe didn't have a driver's license because South Dakota didn't have drivers' licenses. Nobody in Mobridge questioned Black Jack's bride to be. Folks in Mobridge considered Billy Black Bird more white than Indian.

After a steak dinner, Jack introduced Kitty to his cousin Joe. Joe was in awe of the twenty-two-year-old freckled-faced Scottish gal. She had curly reddish hair and an engaging smile. That evening, Kitty taught Joe to dance close and how to roll in the sack. He lost his virginity and fell in love all in the same night.

Sunday, the next day, was entirely devoted to rodeo activities. Jack came in fifth in the bronco-riding event and didn't score at all in bull riding. Billy said to Joe, "I am glad he lost today. It will be easier for him to hang it up." During Sunday evening dinner, Jack announced that he rode in his last rodeo. His parents were going to retire to Mobridge and Billy was going to move out to the ranch. Joe thanked Jack for a great weekend. He got his courage up and said to Billy, "You are a beautiful woman." Jack said, "She is getting better looking in her pregnancy. She will give the McGregor family a son and

160 acres of Indian land." Billy giggled at Jack's projections. He said, "We will expand the family and the ranch."

Kitty put her finishing touches on Joe that night in the sack. Joe aged five years in a short weekend west of the Missouri River. The next morning, Jack dropped Joe off at the train station and drove back to the ranch. Joe immediately fell asleep on the train and woke up to a nudge from the train conductor in Roscoe. He had done a lot of drinking over the weekend and was physically exhausted from too many rolls in the sack with Kitty.

Gertrude picked up Joe at the Milwaukee train depot in Roscoe. She could tell by the slight smirk on Joe's face and a kind of swagger in his walk that the trip to Mobridge was a success.

* * * * *

School was different for Joe this year; he didn't have the companionship of his sister or her tutoring in English lessons. He became bored and restless. Joe played more and more pool and slacked on his homework. His grades dropped dramatically. For the time being, Carl overlooked his son's shortcomings. Joe had very much looked forward to Cathy coming home for Christmas. She disillusioned him on her vacation because she stayed with her girlfriends some nights and other nights went out on a date with Johnny Hoffman. He saw very little of her over Christmas vacation. He had to shoot Sam; Shep went off to die and now he was losing Cathy. Christmas passed and the New Year stormed in from the northwest across the prairies.

Because they didn't milk cows on the farm anymore and no longer raised hogs, there was little need for Joe's help on the farm during the winter months. Carl hauled hay out for the cattle with a front-end loader on the tractor. Joe roomed in the basement of the piano teacher's house in town and drove out to the farm on Fridays after school. On Sunday evenings, he packed clean laundry into his suitcase and pocketed spending money from his mother in preparation for the Monday morning drive to school for the week.

On a Friday during mid-January, a blinding storm moved in. Joe had become fearful of snowstorms, so he asked the principal for permission to leave school early and drive home. He wanted to make sure there was enough daylight to see the road in the blizzard. On the way out of Hosmer, his fears diminished as the storm cleared slightly. About three miles from the farm he experienced whiteouts. He slowed down to five miles per hour and sometimes stopped completely when he couldn't see ditches along the road. He was afraid of dumping the car into the ditch. Darkness could become his real enemy if he had to walk home in the snowstorm. He could follow fence lines with the flashlight, but some land was not fenced. He picked up speed between gusts of wind blowing snow horizontal across the road. Memories of his ride on Sam in a snowstorm floated through his mind. He was alone on this road, and fears of freezing to death in the dark scared him. His parents didn't know he was coming home in the storm. There still was no phone line into Hosmer. After a long, arduous, white-knuckle trip, he saw the cottonwood tree that marked the entrance to the farmyard. He drove next to the house and parked the car. Carl was just leaving the house. He said, "I see you came home early. Now you can help me buck out hay for the cattle." Joe was emotionally and physically drained from the drive. He wanted to punch out the insensitive man.

It stormed all weekend, and Joe was sorry he made the trip out to the farm. He should have stayed in town. At noon on Sunday the storm subsided. Carl told Joe to double chain the Model A and drive to town. He did that, and in the middle of the first hard, windblown snowbank, he stripped the gears in the universal joint. He walked back to the farm and told his dad what had happened to the car. Carl went into a tirade berating Joe unmercifully and told him to walk to town. Carl kept up the reprimand, "Why didn't you know better than to rip out those gears. Now I have to order the parts from Sears and rebuild the universal drive." Joe put on his overshoes, overcoat and stocking cap, took his satchel and starting walking the six miles to town. He crossed many hard-packed snowdrifts that were impassable by car. The walk in quietness gave him three hours to cogitate his future. He concluded that he would definitely leave the farm after he graduated from high school the following year.

He reached Hosmer just as the sun was sliding beyond the horizon, leaving a cold blue sky behind.

* * * * *

Winter transformed into spring on the prairie as it always did. Joe put in full days attending classes and after school plowed with the Farmall M into the darkness of night. His pool hall time was limited to a Saturday evening event. He was anxiously looking forward to summer with no school and the return of Cathy.

Cathy finished her year at Northern State Teachers College and came home for the summer. She announced at the supper table that she had no intention of teaching school. Carl lit into her, "I paid for your year at Northern State Teachers College and now you say that you are not going to teach." Like a liberated female, Cathy quipped, "That's right." Carl wasn't finished with Cathy. He gave his last command, "If you aren't going to teach at our school, I don't want to see you around this farm anymore. Your mother, Joe and I can run this farm without you."

That night, with their bedroom doors ajar, Joe and Cathy carried on their brother-and-sister conversation. Joe vengefully said, "Cathy, you finally caught hell from dad like I have been getting for years. You got a taste of crap that I put up with all the time." "I know. I always felt for you." "Yeah, but you never stood up for me. Mom did." "I am going to get a job and it is not teaching." "I know Cathy. But you won't leave Hosmer. You have the hots for Johnny. Dad likes Johnny but not his religion. His is Catholic." "I'm going to get a job in Minneapolis. Have two contacts there." That night Cathy talked until she heard Joe breathe heavily.

Cathy took the train to Minneapolis and moved in with Johnny Hoffman's sister. Joe worked for his dad though the summer with impunity. His spirits lifted knowing that this would be his last year in school and most probably his last year on the Schultz farm.

Once a month Cathy wrote separate letters to Joe and her mom in an envelope addressed to Joe. Joe promised Cathy that he would not let their mother read letters addressed to him for obvious reasons. Joe and Cathy maintained a private dialogue between themselves. He surmised that she wasn't very happy in Minneapolis from questions she asked about social life around Hosmer. Joe answered her letters, adding in his mother's comments. Gertrude only went to the sixth grade and could read in a limited way, but writing anything beyond a poorly spelled grocery list was perplexing to her.

Joe laughed at Cathy's confession that she had taken up smoking cigarettes. Gertrude and Carl would have had conniptions if they knew that their daughter was puffing on cigarettes. Joe had been smoking on the sly for the past year. His parents recommended that he not smoke but didn't pursue the matter any further. They must have smelled the odor of smoke from his clothes. In post WWII, there were very few men who didn't smoke.

* * * * *

Joe got tired of tying up Pup every morning when he drove off to school. He decided to get rid of Pup. He invited Pup to ride on the fender of the car. The dog was thrilled to make the trip that had been denied him for months. Joe drove up to the senior citizens' home and let Pup jump off. The dog ran up to the front door of the home and waited to be let inside. Joe knew that the residents wanted to adopt Pup. There was an elderly man who said that he would look after Pup. Management appreciated Pup's occasional visits to the home to cheer up the residents. The manager was not in favor of having a dog reside at the home. After school, Joe stopped by the senior citizens' home to check on Pup. He was in the back room with his buddies watching TV. He wagged his tail when Joe addressed him. Pup didn't follow Joe when he walked down the hall past the front desk and out to the car. Joe started the car and drove to the main road, never looking back. He knew that he had pulled off the slickest trick of his life. He hoped that Pup wouldn't be ejected from the senior citizens' home. He prepared himself to answer his mother when she questioned Pup's disappearance.

The next morning, Gertrude asked him what happened to Pup. She knew that the dog had gone to town the day before with Joe. He gave her his explanation. "I left him at the senior citizens' home with Fred. You know Fred. He wanted Pup to stay at the home. He is going to build a doghouse for him, feed him and look after him. Everybody at the home loves him. I stopped by the senior citizens' home after school and Pup didn't want to come home with me." "How do you know that, did you ask him?" "Well, yes, in a manner of speaking." "What are you going to tell Cathy when she finds out that you gave away her dog?" "I will tell her the truth." Joe thought to himself, "So far so good." His mother had to untie the dog every morning after Joe had driven a distance on the road from the farm. Gertrude considered the dog an unnecessary animal on the farm, but tolerated him because he was Cathy's dog.

Joe behaved himself through the winter months. He wasn't involved in any mishaps at school or at home. He was proud that he coasted through his last winter in high school unscathed.

* * * * *

In spring, Joe brought a half-gallon of draft beer to an evening school play practice session. He passed the jug around to the other students. A prissy classmate who never liked Joe tattled to the German Reformed minister, who was still involved with the school, about the beer drinking on school grounds. He got into deep trouble with the minister, his dad and the school board. The minister and his dad decided to expel Joe from school. He was six weeks away from graduating. Carl saw an opportunity to keep Joe from leaving the farm by the failure to graduate. Carl forcefully confronted Joe about his fated future. Joe in anger said, "I don't care what you and that crazy minister have in mind for me. I will take a GED exam and get the hell out of here." Carl uttered his stock rebuttal, "If you leave this farm, you are never to come back. Do you hear?"

Joe went about work on the farm under a constant strain. He avoided the minister through the last days of school. Joe never liked the arrogant minister and now hated the bastard with a passion. His dad stopped harassing him for fear that he would suddenly by impulse leave home. Joe managed to behave himself and graduate with his class.

Chapter XI

Carl had always maintained complete control over the farm and his family with his mother's blessings. Grandma Schultz had died, Cathy left home and his insolent son, who was expected to take over the farm, threatened to run away. Gertrude, his faithful, devoted wife, was all he had left to depend on. Carl was at a loss as to what to do. Gertrude suggested that they offer Joe some land, maybe forty acres, and ten cows in the herd to make him feel part of the farm. Joe pondered the offer but rejected it after considering what life would be like for him living under the control of his domineering father. Carl blew his stack at Joe's refusal. "What more do you want from me? I am trying to give you the farm and you still want to leave." Joe looked away from his father to avoid eye contact and said, "I want to be on my own." He was saying politely that he didn't want anything to do with his father. Later that evening in bed, Gertrude said to Carl, "The problem with you and Joe is that you both are too much alike."

The next morning, Joe gassed up the tractor and started to drive away to work in a field when he heard his dad yell from the corner of the garage by the gas pump. Joe stopped the tractor and dismounted. Joe started to walk toward Carl when he yelled out at Joe, "Get the hell off this farm." Joe was halfway between the parked tractor and his dad when he responded, "The hell with you," did an about face and started to walk back to the tractor. He was about to step on the draw bar and mount the tractor when a log chain stirred up dust and wrapped around his ankles. His father had hurled the chain at him from the back. Joe fell to the ground in severe pain. The tractor was parked on a slight incline and Joe had not set the brakes. Vibrations from the engine caused the tractor to start on a roll down the incline. He reached up, took hold of the draw bar as the tractor picked up momentum and chinned himself up. He got up to the steering wheel and seat. He set the brakes on the tractor. Had he not made it up the tractor, the front wheels would have crushed him while his father was standing petrified only to watch. Joe got off the tractor, picked up the log chain, walked over to his dad and dropped the log chain at his dad's feet. He grabbed him by the throat, cocked his fist and pushed him against the garage door and said, "Don't you dare ever do that again or I'll let you have it." He brought his fist up to dad's face. Carl was white as a sheet and speechless. Joe walked back to the tractor and drove to the hay field and raked hay all day.

The next morning, Joe dressed in clean clothes and drove to Hosmer where he linked up with his friend Mark. Joe told Mark he needed a ride to Aberdeen to see the Army recruiting sergeant. Mark was delighted to drive him to

Aberdeen in his dad's new Buick. Joe presented his high school diploma, birth certificate and draft registration card to the sergeant. He filled out some forms and took a couple of tests. The sergeant asked him where he preferred to take his basic training. He said, "Colorado." The recruiting sergeant sent him to a doctor for a physical and told him to return on Friday. Joe and Mark had a meal with a couple of beers at a local hotel and then drove home.

Gertrude waited up for Joe. With tears in her eyes she asked, "Did you join the Army?" Joe answered, "Yes." "When are you leaving?" "Friday." Oh, my God, it has come to this." "Mom, I can't stay here anymore. You know that. What did you want me to do?" "You could have gone to college like Cathy." "Dad wouldn't let me and you know that. Mom, I want to live my own life. I can't do anything right for him. I have to leave for my sake and his. I thought you would understand that." "You and your dad don't get alone because you are too much alike. I guess you have to do what is best for you. We raised you, taught you right from wrong and now you have to decide things for yourself."

He worked his last day on the farm. On Friday morning, he packed a small suitcase, dressed in his Sunday clothes, sat down at the end of the kitchen table facing his mother as he waited for his friend Mark to pick him up. He attempted to make amends and say goodbye. Gertrude sat at the other end of the table with her hands fingering her shawl and fighting back tears. Joe didn't want to burden his mother any further knowing that his dad would raise hell with her over his joining the Army. Gertrude, in her kind, motherly way, looked up and asked, "You will write?" "Yes." "And you will come home on leave. Maybe for Christmas." "Yes, Mom. I am sorry, Mom." "I know."

Mark arrived. Joe got up and said, "Well, I have to go." He picked up his little suitcase and said, "Good-bye, Mom," walked out of the house and got into the Buick. Mark had the radio turned up high. With a big smile he said to Joe, "We are on our way." Mark spun the wheels as he made a tight turn. Joe looked over his shoulder toward the blacksmith shop and saw his father peeking around the corner of the shop door. The loud radio and Mark's bubbling remarks kept Joe from falling apart emotionally. The reality of finally leaving home hit him hard.

In Aberdeen he was sworn in to serve the United States of America as a soldier. The sergeant handed him a sealed envelope and a bus ticket to Camp Carson at Colorado Springs, Colorado. He and Mark had a Coke at the bus station before he boarded the bus. Mark followed the bus west of Aberdeen, occasionally honking and then turned off at the intersection of the road that led up to Hosmer.

Chapter XII

Joe Schultz became a recruit in the United States Army. They outfitted him with fatigue clothes and a class "A" uniform (dress uniform), an M-1 rifle and all sorts of field gear soldiers drag around with them. Thereafter, every week he received more gear from the company supply room and vaccination shots at the dispensary. In basic training, he attended many classes and marched and marched some more. The drill sergeant ran the men in double time from one place to another and then made them stand around and wait and wait. Beyond training to become a soldier, he learned to do KP, pull guard duty, latrine duty and pull garbage detail. Following mundane orders, abiding by strict discipline and a general regimentation of life was a piece of cake compared to his dad's tyrannical ways.

Joe had to adjust to sleeping in a barracks with thirty other guys who all rose in the morning to a bugle call. On the farm, he rose in his bedroom by the crow of a rooster at sunrise.

He had to learn to live with dysfunctional fellows. Most of the young men were from broken families. Some guys were in trouble with the law and chose the Army over jail time. There were no draftees; everybody had enlisted and was classified as regular Army.

Payday was on the last day of the month before noon. The Army paid in crisp brand-new one, two, five, ten and twenty dollar bills. The rest of the day was off duty for most of the troops. After everyone was paid, the company clerk set up a crap table in the day room. The crap table was an Army blanket stretched across a footlocker. Joe held fresh bills in his left hand, rolled dice with his right, thinking he could learn the game as it progressed. An hour after the game started, he was flat broke. He lost his entire paycheck and the money he brought with him to Camp Carson. The company sharpies cleaned him out fast and unmercifully. That lesson remained indelibly stamped on his mind for the rest of his life. He never rolled dice in a crap game again. Joe learned to roll dice for beers at the pool hall at home. The game these guys played was not a friendly roll of dice from a pillbox for beers. These guys played for blood. It was a peacetime Army with WWII leftover sergeants commanding raw recruits who had come from the lowest level of society. There was no fellowship spirit or much of a buddy system in this peacetime Army. Everyone was on his own trip.

Joe wrote a letter that afternoon to Cathy in Minneapolis asking her for twenty dollars to get him through the month. He needed money for personal hygiene, cigarettes, beer and a weekly movie ticket at the camp theater. A dollar went a long way if a soldier stayed at camp and avoided town. A week went by and Cathy had not responded, so Joe did what other guys did when they were broke. He borrowed twenty dollars from the supply sergeant with a hefty rate of interest. The supply sergeant was a WWII veteran who moonlighted as a supply sergeant and spent most of his time at a hamburger drive-in on the south side of Colorado Springs that he and his wife owned. The supply sergeant was first and foremost an opportunist and businessman. He always dressed in his Class A uniform displaying the Combat Infantry Badge and numerous other ribbons on his chest. He made no bones about his retirement after five more years in the Army.

The supply sergeant told Joe that the first sergeant and his wife were alcoholics. He said, "They are nice people but boozers." The first sergeant was a highly-decorated WWII soldier. Joe liked him because he was sort of a father figure. Joe came to understand why the first sergeant seldom ate lunch and always had a red complexion. It was because of his constant drinking.

After another week went by, Joe received a letter from Cathy postmarked Hosmer, South Dakota. She enclosed a twenty-dollar bill with a long letter explaining that she gave up city life and returned to the farm to help Dad and Mom. She said that Dad welcomed her back since Joe left home to join the Army. Joe knew the real reason she returned to the farm was because of Johnny Hoffman. The letter gave him relief knowing that his parents were not alone on the farm. He had felt guilty for abandoning them. Despite their generous offer of land and cows, he left them for the Army. Now he had Cathy to communicate with and be informed about his dad and mom. Joe had written a letter to his mother but received no answer. His dad refused to answer his letter and his mother wasn't capable of constructing a letter.

Joe paid off his twenty-dollar loan to the supply sergeant with interest. He set up a monthly payroll deduction from his paycheck that went directly into a savings account at the bank in Hosmer. His main objective in joining the Army was to get away from his father and save money for his education at the University of South Dakota after he was discharged from the Army.

Joe finished first in his basic training class. The first sergeant told Joe that he had a high enough IQ to get into Officer's Candidate School at Ft. Benning, Georgia. Lt. Bradford, the company commander, put an end to crap games on payday. He transferred the company clerk out of his unit. The first sergeant had Joe promoted to Private First Class and assigned him to the duty of company clerk. The supply sergeant relied on Joe to fill in for him when he was absent. The first sergeant asked Joe to cover for him when he was not feeling well, hung over, in other words. Joe and a platoon sergeant pretty much ran the company for Lt. Bradford, the company commander. Joe saw a lot of the lieutenant because of the increasing absences of the first sergeant. Lt. Bradford promoted Joe to corporal.

The lieutenant engaged Joe in a personal conversation about Joe's life. He asked, "Why did you enlist?" Joe answered, "I had to get away from my dad." Lt. Bradford said, "That's partly the reason most men enlist in the Army these days." Lt. Bradford suggested that Joe either apply for Adjutant General school or apply for OCS and become an infantry officer. Joe quickly explained, "I am not a career soldier."

Lt. Bradford said, "I started out as a career officer but am about to change that. I am tired of this peacetime Army. Can't get promoted. Have to train a bunch of misfits with WWII goof-off sergeants. I have a degree in engineering from the Point. My wife has a master's degree in education. She teaches in Colorado Springs and doesn't ever want to leave Colorado." "Sir, I don't understand the Point." "Oh, that's West Point. I graduated from the Army's military college. I have a regular Army commission."

Joe said, "I am saving money to attend the university after my enlistment is up." The lieutenant asked, "Where did you grow up?" "South Dakota." Lt. Bradford rose to leave his office and said, "I wish you well." Joe stood up and suggestively said, "Sir, I would like to become the company supply sergeant some day." "In due time, I will do that for you. Corporal, keep this conversation under your hat." "Yes, sir." "I am going into town to goof off like the other guys in this peacetime army. I never expected a peacetime army to be so sloppy. See you tomorrow, corporal."

Lt. Bradford realized his dream when war broke out in Korea in June 1950. President Harry Truman called it a police action. For men in the infantry, it soon would become a full-scale war. Lt. Bradford volunteered for duty in Korea after he finished paratrooper school. The lieutenant joyfully set out to clean house before his departure. He forced the first sergeant into a medical discharge and placed the supply sergeant's name on a levy for duty in Korea. He promoted the senior platoon sergeant to first sergeant of the company. He promoted Joe to the rank of staff sergeant in the position of company supply sergeant.

Life changed quickly at Camp Carson after war broke out in Korea. A captain, an activated reserve officer, became Joe's new company commander. A green second lieutenant, a Reserve Officer Training Cadet, was transferred in and became the new platoon officer. Draftees started to trickle in for basic training. Camp Carson took on a WWII look overnight. The 196th Regimental Combat Team (RCT), South Dakota National Guard, was activated. They arrived at Camp Carson and moved into barracks that had been vacant since WWII. Camp Carson was bustling with new faces. The 196th RCT was at partial strength and soon would be at full strength as draftees arrived every week. Camp Carson became a training center that took civilians and turned them into soldiers in a couple of months. After draftees finished basic training, they were shipped straight to battlefields in Korea.

To Joe's knowledge, he had been the only soldier from South Dakota in Camp Carson until the 196th RCT arrived. He hustled up to the PX near the 196th RCT Headquarters, bought a beer and sat down with two sergeants wearing the crest of the 196th RCT. He introduced himself as a native from Hosmer, South Dakota. This took the two South Dakota National Guard sergeants by surprise. They told Joe that they were from Pierre, South Dakota. One of the sergeants was assigned to a reconnaissance platoon in Headquarters and Headquarters Company and the other sergeant was in Service Company assigned to Regimental S-4 (Supply). The National Guard supply sergeant introduced himself as Sgt. Brown and his friend as Sgt. Downing. Sgt. Schultz introduced himself to his two new friends as a company supply sergeant in a regular Army training regiment down the street. Sgt. Brown immediately asked Joe to transfer to the 196th RCT so he could join him at regimental supply. Joe was overwhelmed at the request. He had served with flunkies for over two years and now had the opportunity to serve with a couple of guys from South Dakota. Joe said, "I don't know if that's possible." The two sergeants from Pierre said that they could arrange that, they had connections. Joe soon learned that the South Dakota National Guard was like a big family; they all looked out for each other and the only difference between non-commissioned and commissioned officers was rank with respect.

Staff in all the training regiments and camp headquarters worked seven days a week processing incoming draftees. Three weeks had passed since Joe had met with his friends from Pierre. He wandered up to the 196th RCT PX in search of his South Dakota friends. He found the regimental supply sergeant having a Coors beer with a PFC and corporal at a picnic table. Joe noticed that the regimental supply sergeant had been promoted from sergeant first class to the rank of master sergeant. It took Joe two years to make the rank of staff sergeant and Sgt. Brown was promoted to the rank of master sergeant after having been on active duty for only two months. Joe had been soldiering in a peacetime army and Sgt. Brown was promoted in wartime conditions. Military life changed at a quick pace after the Korean War broke out.

Joe asked Sgt. Brown the whereabouts of Sgt. Downing. He answered, "Oh, he went home to get his car." Joe asked what he and Sgt. Downing did before they were activated. Sgt. Brown answered, "I completed my freshman year and Downing finished his second year at the university." Sgt. Brown asked Sgt. Schultz, "Are you ready to transfer into my unit?" Joe cleared his throat and said, "I am afraid it's too late for that. I am shipping out. Have orders to go to Korea. I am leaving camp tomorrow. Going on two weeks leave and then on to Korea." Sgt. Brown said, "You are going to Korea. If you had transferred to 196th RCT, you could have stayed stateside for the rest of your enlistment. I could have arranged that. I have connections. We are staying in Camp Carson as a training regiment." Joe tilted his head, smiled and said, "Thank you just the same. It's time I earned my sergeant's pay. On to Korea it is." The two soldiers shook hands and vowed that they would see each other again.

* * * * *

Joe rode on a Greyhound bus into South Dakota and then transferred to a Jack Rabbit Bus that took him to Bowdle. The Schultz farm was still isolated because it had no phone to town. Joe called his buddy Mark in Hosmer for a ride home from Bowdle. Thirty minutes later, Mark arrived in a blue Buick. Joe tossed his duffle bag into the back seat of the car and said, "I see you are still driving your dad's Buick." Mark said, "It's mine now. Dad gave it to me for school. I am a sophomore at the university this year." Joe said, "I take it that you are home for Thanksgiving vacation." "Yes. I'm glad that I didn't miss you on your leave." "Mark, I am on leave because I have orders for Korea." "Holy smoke, you are going to Korea." "Yes."

There were times in past years when Joe thought everything in South Dakota stood still and nothing ever changed. Life was changing on the prairies while he was gone. He asked Mark, "What are those poles along the road?" Mark said, " Those are power poles that will carry REA electricity to all the farmers. They are going to string a phone line on the same poles. Farmers will be able to make long-distance phone calls to anywhere in the world." "I wrote a note to Cathy telling her that I was on my way home but don't know if she has received it by now." "So Cathy doesn't know you are coming home." "I don't know. Nobody knows that I am on my way to Korea."

Mark pulled into the Schultz farmyard and parked by the house. Joe said to Mark, as he took his duffle bag from the back seat of the car, "Thanks for the ride. I will see you in town." Joe took his duffle bag into the house and then walked toward the garage. He saw Cathy's car parked in the garage, but the pickup was gone. He heard a hum coming from down south of the farm. It was Cathy and her mother pulling a trailer with the small Allis Chalmer tractor. They stopped digging potatoes and headed home when they saw Joe get out of Mark's car. They were surprised at Joe's unexpected arrival. After shaking hands and exchanging a few pleasantries, Gertrude suggested they go inside the house. Joe asked, "Where is Dad?" Cathy said, "He is in Aberdeen buying tires for the truck and the cars. He fears a Korean War shortage." "What is that hole by the garage?" "Ho! He is going to bury another 300-gallon gasoline tank. He is afraid gasoline will be rationed because of the war." War was on Joe's mind because very soon he'd be in the middle of it in Korea. He looked at his mom and said, "Mom, I am on my way to Korea." Gertrude removed her shawl, sat down at the kitchen table and started to wring her hands. She said, "I was afraid of this when I saw you get out of Mark's car. When are you going?" "In two weeks when my leave is up." He asked Cathy, "Did you receive my letter telling you that I was coming home?" "No. Did you send it to our Hillsview address?" "Yes." "A lot of things have changed since you where home the last time. The train doesn't come up from Roscoe anymore. Everything comes to town by truck. The post office in Hillsview closed down. The town just died. Our mail now comes to Hosmer. Soon we will have 110-volt electricity and a phone line to town on those REA poles." "Mark told me about the power poles." Folks drive to Aberdeen to buy clothes, refrigerators, stoves, washing machines, cars and everything else."

Joe couldn't fathom the train not rolling up from Roscoe to Strasburg. It took him a week to comprehend the changes that had taken place in his absence. In town there used to be two car dealerships, and now there was one and it was failing. There used to be three creameries in Hosmer, and now there was one. None of the farmers were milking cows. Milk was produced in dairies; chicken and eggs came from chicken farms. Farmers were buying electric motors to replace their Briggs and Stratton gasoline engines in anticipation of REA power.

Carl drove into the yard with a pickup load of tires. Joe went to greet him. Carl got out of the truck and said, "I see you made it back. Change your clothes and help me unload these tires." Carl Schultz had not changed. He was the same single-minded man he had always been. He didn't even offer Joe a handshake.

At dinner that night, Carl explained the merits of the Korean War. He said that President Truman started this war to pull the country out of a post WWII economic slump. As usual, Carl had all this analyzed and figured out in his mind. Carl was living proof of the president's economic theory. He bought all those extra tires, was going to double his gasoline storage, bought a new Oldsmobile and built a single-car garage by the house for the car, all because he feared shortages. Carl was stimulating the economy with his purchases.

The next day Joe and Cathy drove to town on an excursion trip to be away from the farm. Cathy let Joe drive her car. She was driving the former family car, a sage- colored 1949 Ford. Her Model A Ford was parked behind the Model T Ford truck by Sam's grave. Joe enjoyed driving the car. Over the past two years, Joe didn't drive a car, truck or tractor; he rode in the back of six-by-six Army trucks at camp or rode a bus into Colorado Springs. In Hosmer they talked to people that Joe had not seen since he had left for the Army. One blond crew-cut, former WWII Marine jarhead asked Joe, "Where have you been?" Joe, standing before him in uniform, answered, "The Army. I am on my way to Korea." The meathead responded, "Oh yeah. That police action in Korea." Joe nudged Cathy in the shoulder and started to walk away from the WWII hero. Joe said, "I am sorry I came home on leave before shipping out." "Joe, Mom and I would never have forgiven you." They stopped at the drugstore to have an ice-cream soda and indulged in nostalgia about their childhood days. Walking to the car, Cathy motioned toward the ex-Marine and said, "You know that blowhard never was overseas, he never saw combat, he was a drill instructor during WWII.

At the supper table, Carl was his old self, lecturing how he can make lots of money due to higher wheat prices because of the war, but he needed Joe at home to help him out on the farm. He was going to buy more land, one more tractor, a dual-wheeled dump truck and a new self-propelled combine. Carl had checked out the possibility of getting Joe a hardship discharge from the Army because he was an only son of a farmer. Joe politely interrupted and said, "Dad, I am going to finish what I started. It is my duty to go to Korea and fight Communism." Carl got all puffed up and said, "Well, damn you and go. See if I care. Have it your way. Don't ever come back to this farm while I am alive." The Schultz lord and master had spoken and said more or less, "Come back over my dead body." This was déjà vu all over again, like two and a half years ago when he left for the Army. Joe knew that should he take a discharge from the Army and return to the farm, his father would have him firmly imprisoned without parole. He cut his leave short and asked Cathy to take him to Bowdle the next day to catch a bus. He had orders to fly from Denver to Seattle and then on to Japan.

He put his duffle bag in the trunk of the car and seated himself in the passenger side. Cathy looked over her shoulder as they passed the blacksmith shop. Joe looking straight ahead said, "When I left for the Army he peeked around the shop door." Cathy laughed and said, "He just did it again."

At the bus station, they made small talk waiting for the bus to arrive. Cathy said to Joe, "You didn't get to see Johnny." "How is Johnny?" "He's fine. We would like to get married but you know Dad." "Screw him. Get married anyway. Johnny is a first- class guy. Tell him I said so." Joe gave Cathy a hug and boarded the bus. Cathy cried as the bus roared off into the west.

* * * * *

In Denver, Joe decided to return to Camp Carson and use up his last week of leave. He arrived at camp and checked in with his former first sergeant and asked for permission to visit Camp Hale for R & R. Camp Hale had been the training camp for the 10th Mountain Infantry during WWII and now was a military rest camp. Joe rode on an Army bus to Camp Hale. The camp was nestled up high in the Rocky Mountains. He did some fly-fishing, hiking and slept like a log in a barracks by a gurgling stream that flowed through the middle of Camp Hale. He fell in love with the Rocky Mountains all over again. He decided to return to Colorado as a civilian if he survived Korea. He developed second thoughts about his trip overseas. The guys at the 196th RCT had offered him an alternative to Korea. His father could have kept him on the farm, but he opted to pay his dues to the U.S.A as a soldier.

After three days of R & R, the Army bus took him back to Camp Carson and dropped him off in front of his former barracks. He found a bunk and set his duffel bag next to it. He walked to a PX near the 196th RCT Headquarters in search of his two friends from Pierre. Two Coors beer trucks were churning up dust behind the PX. South Dakota National Guard men and midwestern draftees had given up their taste for their hometown beers like Schmidt's, Schlitz, Budweiser, Millers and Pabst Blue Ribbon for Coors, that Colorado mountain beer bottled in Golden, Colorado. The guys in the 196th RCT loved their beer. They guzzled it by the truckloads. Joe couldn't find his friends because they were out on a bivouac. The next morning, without seeing his friends, he left Camp Carson for Stapleton Airport in Denver and boarded a Pan Am flight to Seattle and then on to Japan. In a couple of days, he was in Korea. The Army was extremely efficient in getting troops to the front lines. He was assigned to Divisional Headquarters in the supply section.

In his first letter to Cathy from Korea, he said, "This place is chaotic. I have been confused from the day I arrived. The saying around here is that a situation is normal when it is all screwed up. Army Information and Education quoted

General McArthur to say that the "police action" in Korea will be wrapped up by Christmas. Everybody believes General McArthur. He is the only man besides Jesus Christ who ever walked on water, so they say.

Chinese troops came across the northern Korean border in hordes, and the predicted Christmas victory turned into a living nightmare. United Nations forces were overrun by the Chinese and North Korean troops. Many U.S. soldiers were killed, maimed and captured in their attempted retreat. Divisional Headquarters became the front lines because they couldn't move out fast enough. Shovels, bayonets, canteens, K rations, gasoline tanks, rifles, artillery guns and ammunition were left behind in hasty retreat. China was long on manpower and short on war materiel. Chinese soldiers took captured American equipment and used it creatively. They made hand grenades out of empty K ration tin cans. Chinese soldiers fired at Americans with guns and ammo that was left behind by the U.S. troops.

Christmas was a miserable time for the foot soldier in the dark, bleak and depressing place called Korea. Dinner was served from mess trucks to guys standing in line with their mess kits in hand for turkey and mashed potatoes with gravy. The bland, haphazard prepared meal froze from the bottom up in the aluminum mess kit. Hot coffee poured into the aluminum cup burned their lips and quickly turned ice cold.

Supposedly, United Nations troops fought the North Koreans and Chinese. That was a farce. U.S. forces fought the war against Communism. WWII veterans who were running the United States in Washington, D. C., feared a domino effect in the spread of Communism in Asia should Korea fall into the enemy hands. The Korean War was supported by politicians who were misguided by high-ranking military brass. Foot soldiers hated this war, and the general population at home was ambivalent about it.

* * * * *

A month after that dreadful Christmas, Sgt. Schultz's division began to retreat southward when Chinese troops broke through the front lines. Sgt. Schultz and his supply unit were loading what they could into the few trucks available to them when they noticed a momentary silence. The artillery firing subsided. Their artillery was pulling out and retreating to the south. Joe deserted the master sergeant and warrant officer in charge of Divisional Supply and joined the other troops in retreat. He spotted a jeep behind the headquarters tent with a general sitting at the steering wheel. The general looked dazed. Joe asked him if he wanted him to drive the jeep. The general rolled his eyes and mumbled incoherently. Joe didn't know what to do on the spur of the moment. He thought to pull the general out off the jeep and drive south by himself. A private double-timed toward him and asked,

"Do you need help?" Joe said to the private, "Yes. Help me move this guy into the passenger side. I don't know what is wrong with him, but he sure is out of it." The private dropped his rifle and the two pulled the fat, bald- headed general out of the driver's seat and managed to drag him around the jeep and lift him into the passenger seat. The private said to Joe, "He is having a heart attack. I know. I was a med student at Stanford." Joe told the private to jump into the back of the jeep, place his rifle down alongside the general as a guard to keep him from tumbling out of the jeep. Joe drove full tilt down the road to a wide spot that had a red cross on the side of a tent. It was a Mobile Army Surgical Hospital (MASH) unit. The little red flag with a star in the middle mounted on the left fender of the jeep got the attention of the men at the MASH unit. A captain triaged the general and said, "He is having a heart attack." They moved the general inside and debriefed Joe in the orderly room. Joe told them about the retreat that was coming south. He gave them his version of the rescue of the general. The private had disappeared into a bus loaded with wounded men destined to an Army hospital down south.

Joe asked for permission to take a shower and be assigned a cot to sleep on. He had not showered in days. After his shower, he fell into an Army cot and slept for twelve hours. He awoke famished. He made two trips though the chow line in the mess tent. The company clerk entered the mess tent and yelled, "Sergeant Schultz." Joe answered, "Here."

The company clerk said, "You lucky dog are going home. Emergency leave. Your father died." Joe swallowed hard, reached for his cup of coffee and tried to digest the corporal's message. He caught a ride on the next Army bus that went south to an air base. He received his travel orders attached to a "201 File," his military personnel file, and boarded a military flight to Japan. In Japan he flew Pan Am to Seattle and was discharged from the Army at Ft. Lawton in Seattle. He called home from Seattle and found out that his dad had died two weeks ago. Cathy said, "Dad had a massive heart attack. We had the funeral not knowing when you would come home. They said that you were missing in action." "I am coming home for good. They gave me a hardship discharge because of Dad's death." Cathy said, "That's great. I can't wait to see you. Mom has been worried sick ever since you went to Korea."

Joe flew to Denver and boarded a bus for the last leg of his trip to South Dakota. In Pierre he had lunch, called Cathy to let her know that he would be in Bowdle before nightfall. He transferred to a bus that would take him to Selby. Half way to Selby it started to snow. At Selby, he was supposed to transfer to another bus that was coming in from Mobridge and went through Bowdle. There was a short wait between his arrival in Selby and departure for the bus coming in from Mobridge. The wind suddenly came up and a blizzard quickly turned into a South Dakota whiteout.

The bus station in Selby was the home of an elderly couple. They were the ticket agents for the bus company. The husband said to Joe, "Bus won't come through today. You will have to stay here tonight and catch the bus in the morning." He had come all the way from a combat zone in Korea to South Dakota without a hitch and now was snowbound so close to home. They showed him the bathroom and asked him to have supper with them. Joe slept in the cold porch on a cot. During the middle of the night, he woke up in a cold sweat. He had his first nightmare since leaving Korea. Next morning the sun came out and there was fresh snow everywhere. During breakfast with the elderly couple, the husband asked Joe where he had been stationed. He told them that he had been in Korea and was on his way to home to Hosmer. That was the extent of their conversation during his stay with them. Joe felt uncomfortable being isolated in this house with a couple that tolerated him as an inconvenience. He was relieved when he heard the bus roaring up to the front of the house. He thanked the elderly couple for their hospitality and boarded the bus to Bowdle.

He disembarked in Bowdle and called Cathy at the farm. One hour later, Cathy arrived in the Oldsmobile to pick up her hero. She no longer referred to him as her little brother; he had grown into manhood, a decorated Korean veteran. He wore a Combat Infantry Badge and battle ribbons on the chest of his uniform. He had become her big brother. Cathy said to Joe as they by passed Hosmer, "We can go visit Dad's grave tomorrow with Mom. Right now she wants to see you. She worried over you every day while you were in Korea." "Why didn't she come with you?" "I think she was afraid of crying in front of people in Bowdle."

Cathy drove up to the new garage Carl had built for the Oldsmobile. Gertrude was standing outside the front door of the house waiting. She had been sitting by the window in the house for two hours waiting for the Oldsmobile to come up the road. Joe got out of the car and hugged her. She broke down and cried. Joe and his mother had never hugged each other before. Joe broke the embrace and looked at the blacksmith shop and garage foundations covered with sod and ashes. He asked, "What happened?" His mother said, "We go in and I tell you everything."

Gertrude told him that his dad had been welding with the arc welder, had a massive heart attack and died. Presumably, he dropped the welding torch near oil-soaked rags and fire ensued. When Cathy saw smoke bellowing from the blacksmith shop, she rushed to the shop and pulled Carl out of the fire. She said, "He was dead when I got him out. Within minutes the oil-soaked blacksmith shop just blew up like a bomb. A northwest breeze blew flames from the blacksmith shop against the garage. I backed out the car and truck first and then backed out the tractor. That's when the upstairs of the garage blew apart. I just barely backed the tractor away from the garage before it blew up. Dad had stored paint, oil cans and empty gasoline cans in the upstairs of the garage." Joe said, "Reminds me of napalm bombs the Air Force dropped on the enemy in Korea." "When the north end of the upstairs blew out, the roof fell in and the garage burned to the ground in minutes. Nothing happened to the underground gasoline tanks." Joe looked at what was his father's favorite place, the blacksmith shop, and said, "Well, he died doing what he enjoyed the most, working in the blacksmith shop." Cathy said, "And do you know what? He didn't have a cent of insurance." Joe said, "That doesn't surprise me a bit. The only insurance he ever bought was hail insurance on wheat crops."

The next day they drove to town and visited Carl's grave. It was an agonizing experience for Joe. He joined the Army to get away from his dad and now was discharged from the Army and came home because of him. His father more or less had said, "Return over my dead body." Joe standing at the foot of his father's grave pondered how things could have been different if he and his father had had a real father-son relationship, what if? He felt guilty that he didn't try harder to get along with his father. He consoled himself that the past is the past and nothing can change that. Cathy nudged her mother and said, "Let's not dwell on the dead, life is for the living." Her mother nodded and said, "We go downtown and see folks."

Joe saw a freshly dug grave in the northwestern part of the cemetery. He broke the silence and asked, "That freshly dug grave over there, did they bury another Jew?" Cathy said, "Oh, no. They dug up that Jewish doctor who was here during WWII. He died and they buried him over there. They dug him up and shipped him to a Jewish cemetery in Minneapolis." "May I guess whose idea that was?" Cathy said, "Our minister got people stirred up because they had buried a Jew in this Protestant cemetery." Joe said, "That figures." Cathy stopped walking and addressed Joe directly, "Don't be so hard on the German Reformed minister. He helped Mom and I contact you in Korea."

Joe shook his head and looked up at the cold blue sky. It was the end of January, the month of his birthday, the month when bad things happened to him. He said to his mother, "I'm sorry I missed Dad's funeral." Cathy smiled and said, "Yeah, but you will be here for my wedding." "When is that?" "A week from Saturday. Will you give me away?" He smiled back and said, "My pleasure. Are you getting married in Hoffman's Catholic Church?" "No. We compromised. Johnny and I are getting married in the Lutheran Church. We invited everybody in town to our wedding dance. It should be one big party. We also can celebrate your homecoming." Joe said, "I will never set foot in that German Reformed Church ever again." Gertrude abruptly said, "Don't talk that way. Your dad was the church treasurer. He paid your church dues all the years you were away." Joe pulled his hands out of his pockets and led the way back to the car.

They wandered around town and visited folks. There was much to talk about, Carl Schultz's death, Joe's return from Korea and the general local subjects that were standard gossip. Their last stop in town was at the senior citizens' home. Pup got all excited when he saw Cathy and her mother. Pup licked Joe's hand like he licked everyone's hand. Cathy said to Joe, "I hated you for leaving Pup here. Now I am happy he is here for the senior citizens." Folks at the home welcomed Joe and thanked him for giving Pup to them. They loved their four-legged bundle of joy.

On the way home, Joe decided to tell his mother about his future plans. He said to Cathy, in hopes that his mother was listening, "Now that you and Johnny are getting married and will farm the land, I plan to enroll at the university this fall." Cathy burst out, "I was planning on that." Gertrude wasn't in agreement with Joe's plans but kept her thoughts to herself. She was happy to have her family together again and hoped someday Joe would come back to the Schultz farm.

Chapter XIII

Cathy and Johnny got married in grand fashion. The Hoffman clan made the wedding a family affair. They all participated and that pleased Gertrude very much. Johnny and Cathy had been dating on the sly for years and recently openly despite Carl. The Hoffman boys were happy that their youngest brother finally got married to his one and only girlfriend. Folks from all around Hosmer gathered for the Saturday night hoedown.

Gertrude had to adjust to the loss of her husband, a son who returned home and a son-in-law who moved in with the family. Joe took to civilian life quickly but was plagued with nightmares. He fixed fences, picked rocks and did odd jobs for mental therapy. Years ago, as a young man on the farm, he hated picking rocks and fixing fences.

Joe discussed his lack of funds for four years at the university with his mother. She said, "Don't worry about money, I give you some. And, I told Cathy to give you her car." She put Joe's mind at ease. Cathy's car was the former family car, the 1949 Ford. Cathy and Gertrude drove the new Oldsmobile and Johnny had a new Chrysler. Joe mailed a copy of his discharge and a letter requesting admission to the university. They responded positively.

By the time fall came, Joe had rehabilitated to civilian life thanks to Johnny who was like a big brother to him. Johnny had vicarious war experiences through his brothers who were in service during WWII. One brother was killed, another brother had part of his leg shot off, and the two older brothers were unscathed by the war. Johnny helped Joe adapt to civilian life.

September came and Joe prepared for his new life as a student at the University of South Dakota in Vermillion. The night before his departure to Vermillion, the family had a pleasant discussion at the supper table unlike the monologues by the infallible Carl Schultz. Joe suggested that Gertrude retire to town. She said, " I stay here. Feed my chickens and help out when the baby comes. A boy." Joe dropped the subject because it wasn't any of his business what took place on the Schultz farm. He had divorced himself from the farm when he joined the Army.

Joe had adjustments to make in his life at school. He was in classes with eighteen-year-old young men who were on their own for the first time. Joe, at the age of twenty-two felt like a thirty-year-old man around little boys. He was one of the first Korean veterans to enroll at the university. WWII veterans had been there and were long gone. The other challenge was his poor high school education and the four-year gap between high school and the present. Young boys who were fresh out of big high schools from Sioux Falls breezed through their courses. Joe studied and lived with his books day and night. He was on probation until midterm and maybe the end of first semester. If his grades were below a certain level, he would have to leave the university. Professors willingly gave him extra help because he was a Korean veteran with determination.

Joe struggled with Psychology 101. He learned that he had an ego and was exposed to Dr. Ivan Pavlov's experiment in conditioned reflexes. Dr. Pavlov rang a bell and then fed his little dog. He did this over a period of time and then stopped that routine. He would ring the bell but not feed the dog. The dog salivated when he heard the bell that signaled chow time. This experiment proved the theory of conditioned reflexes for Dr. Pavlov. That about summed up what Joe learned in Psych 101. He was placed in a refresher English class, remedial English. He was in a class with other guys who couldn't spell or comprehend what they read. His counselor advised him to sign up for a speech class. He had the shock of his life on the first day in speech class. The professor made every student in class read a few lines into a tape recorder and then played it back for the entire class to hear. Joe was embarrassed to hear his heavy German accent. He thought that he had a slight accent but nothing like what he heard played back on the tape recorder. Now he realized why sergeants in senior rank to him teasingly called him Sergeant Kraut. Joe's objective in speech class was to rid himself of the German accent.

The dean of the school of business gave Joe a jolt when he called him to appear before him in his office a week before midterm. The dean taught Economics 101 to the freshmen pre-business class. He was a pompous, gray-haired man, who wore chrome-rimmed glasses, a handkerchief in the vest pocket and a red rose in the lapel of his gray suit. He was like the character Mr. Babbitt in Sinclair Lewis's novel.

Joe feared that he was about to receive his walking orders from the university. He made his appearance at the dean's office upon request. Joe stood at attention holding his books in his left hand, leaving his right hand free to salute the big man, a general in his mind at the time. The dean's secretary seated to the left of him rose and handed him a blue book containing the answers to a quiz Joe had written in class two days prior. The dean said, "You used the word entrepreneur eleven times in this quiz and misspelled it eleven times. That's not what bothers me. You misspelled the word differently nine times. Are you enrolled in refresher English." Joe startled the dean when he answered loudly, "Yes, sir." The dean looked up and saw a young man wearing a crew haircut, Army pile jacket and standing at attention. In a parting look he said to Joe, "That's all." Joe did a military about-face and went to his next class. He was relieved to know he had not been rejected from the university. Several times during the semester he thought he wouldn't make it to midterm. The first two and a half months at the university were like basic training in the Army. Everything at school was a new adventure for Joe. He had lost faith in himself and then regained it again at midterm. He drove home for the Thanksgiving break a young man who had changed from farmer to soldier and now to student.

* * * * *

Gertrude received a surprise letter in the mail from the Internal Revenue Service requesting to meet with her and discuss unpaid income taxes. Carl had told her once that if he didn't file to pay income taxes with the IRS they would never know he existed. He assured her that it would all work out fine. He said, "None of the other farmers are filing so it must be okay." Gertrude seldom questioned her husband because he was always right. Joe and Cathy accompanied their mother to the lion's den, as Joe referred to the IRS guys. The federal agent had all the receipts from grain elevators and livestock sale barns dating back to WWII with Carl Schultz's name on them. He had a total of unpaid taxes due with accrued interest and penalties for failure to file with the IRS. The agent had allowed a reasonable amount for expenses against the total sale of wheat and cattle over the years. He gave Gertrude the opportunity to contest the total of $10,000 due. Cathy said to her mother, "Mom, write the check." Gertrude was slightly shocked. "How much did he say?" The agent politely said, "I rounded off the amount to $10,000 with the understanding that you pay that amount today without contest." Cathy said, "It looks fair to me, Mom. Write the check."

Joe walked the twenty-acre field north of the farmyard to hunt pheasants. He stopped where old machinery was parked by Sam's grave. The rock that he had placed to mark Sam's grave was still there. Next to the grave was the single share plow used by his great grandfather to bust sod on the twenty acres he was about to walk and hunt. The plow had an oak beam attached to the plowshare on one end and a metal hitch on the other end. His great grandfather had used two oxen to turn the soil on the twenty acres of the homestead. Sam's grave brought back boyhood memories. He walked the perimeter around the twenty-acre field back to Sam's grave. He heard a pheasant rooster cackle and then he flew along the fence line into the setting sun. There always had been a family of pheasants living along the north fence line of the farmyard among the scrubs and bushes. Joe wondered when pheasants first settled in this particular habitat. He walked past the house down to the southern border of the farmyard behind the garage to a small slough. He wanted to see if the covey of partridges still lived there. They did. He raised his gun but couldn't get a shot off. The covey flew a short distance west and landed by the cottonwood tree. He had never killed a partridge, never even winged one. He shouldered the gun and walked back to the house.

At the end of Thanksgiving break, Joe drove back to school, and a month later returned home again for Christmas vacation. He made very few trips to town over Christmas vacation. He studied hard for semester finals in January, and those efforts paid off with passing grades. He got a C- in Physiology, C in Western Civilization, B- in Refresher English, B- in Algebra and a C in Economics 101. He assured himself that he would get a degree from the school of business some day. He stayed in Vermillion over spring break and studied. On afternoons he would sneak off to road hunt pheasants. He gave the pheasants he shot to his landlady and the woman who did his laundry every week. Joe's grade average rose slightly from the first semester to the second semester.

At the end of the second semester, Joe returned to the farm for more mental therapy. His help wasn't needed on the farm. Johnny and his brothers accomplished more in a week on the farm with their large equipment than the Schultz family did in an entire month. Johnny simplified the farm to raising wheat, cattle and, of course, Gertrude had her chickens and ducks. Joe spent less time working on the farm and more time with his friend Mark in Hosmer that summer. Mark was to be a senior and Joe a sophomore this fall at the university.

* * * * *

Joe's return to school in the fall of 1952 was a pleasure. He had learned how to study in his freshman year and had become campus-wise. He knew his way around the library and different buildings that housed the various departments of government, English, history and mathematics. Joe's social life took a turn for the better when his buddies from Pierre showed up at the university. He enjoyed having a beer at the campus watering hole with them and other Korean veterans. There was hardly any dating for a veteran who was not a Greek, that is, a member of a fraternity. Veterans devoted themselves to studying and drinking a few beers on weekends. The male-to-female ratio on campus was five to one. Even frat boys had trouble getting dates sometimes. Many girls enrolled at the university to find a husband. Occasionally, Joe and his supply sergeant friend, J. B. Brown, drove to Yankton on Saturday evenings to dance and cavort with working girls in that town. Former Sergeant Brown in civilian life went by the name of J.B. Brown and the Sergeant Downing was John Downing. The three guys palled around on weekends, taking in football games and special events.

The Dakota Day parade was a special event. A cowboy held a coyote on a leash on top of a delivery van. Supposedly, the coyote was tame but he looked like he wanted to jump off the van and make his escape. The coyote was the University of South Dakota mascot. The homecoming queen, a pretty sorority girl, sat on her throne on the next float. All the fraternities and sororities proudly paraded their beautifully decorated floats except the Phi Deltas. Their float was innovative with an artistic approach, but crude in taste.

A fraternity brother sat in a one-hole old outhouse on the flatbed of an old farm truck. His pants were down to his ankles and he cradled a roll of toilet paper on his lap. He sat in the position of The Thinker, a statue by Rodin. He rested his right elbow on his knee and cupped his chin with that hand. His left hand rested on his left thigh. On top of the outhouse was a plaque that read, "Tchaikovsky's Last Movement."

After the parade Joe, J.B. and John went for hamburgers and beer. J.B. suggested that Joe visit the library on Tuesday or Thursday afternoons and look at Miss South Dakota's beautiful legs. J.B. knew from past visits that she studied in the library on those days in the afternoon. Joe said that he would read the comic strip in the afternoon instead of in the morning at the library. The dean of the school of business recommended to his class in Econ 101 to read Dick Tracy, Pogo, Little Abner, Peanuts and Little Orphan Annie. Joe got into the habit of reading the comic strips because of the Dean's suggestion. After lunch they walked over to the ball field to watch the university lose. They seldom won a football game. Waiting for the game to start, Joe told the story about the Phi Delta dog that roamed around campus freely. He was the only dog on campus and probably the only dog in town. On the first day of an econ class the professor introduced himself as Dryer and said that his lectures were even drier. In the middle of the lecture, the Phi Delta dog, a large brown German shepherd, walked into the classroom, lay down and fell asleep. The class started to giggle and move around in their seats. When the class bell rang, the dog got up and left the building to mix with students outside.

Joe rented a sleeping room from a family two blocks beyond the Phi Delta house. He walked past the Phi Delta house on his way to the campus everyday. Joe told J.B. and John that on sunny winter days the Phi Delta dog sunned himself in the doorway of the fraternity house. Phi Deltas seldom closed the front door of their house and during the spring and fall they left the back door open. Joe could see right through the middle of the house from front to back. Joe said that an upper classman told him that a Phi Delta shower was body powder sprinkled across the back and up the armpits. The Phi Delta house consisted of delightful rough guys who had a lot of character. Members of the fraternity were mostly jocks who played on the school's basketball and football teams.

The following Tuesday afternoon, Joe went to the library to read the comics and see Miss South Dakota's legs. Joe saw a beautiful, blue-eyed blond studying at a table in the middle of the reading room in the library. He wasn't very sophisticated in judging a woman's anatomy. He looked at her face and stopped at her breasts. She was the most beautiful woman Joe had ever seen on campus. He assumed she must be Miss South Dakota. Joe's goggling at Miss South Dakota in the library was short-lived. Two weeks later he didn't see her in the library anymore. J.B. said she had left school with Casey Tibbs.

* * * * *

During the second semester of his sophomore year, Joe discovered that, for the first time in his life, he was thinking in English and speaking and writing in English. He had labored all his life thinking in German and expressing himself in English. Studying came easier, and his grade average rose dramatically. He finished his second year at the university and returned to the Schultz farm for the summer.

In the fall, his third year in school, Joe enrolled in the school of business. He went to see the dean for advice on what electives to take in the fall semester. Joe had not been in to see the dean since he was called on the carpet for misspelling entrepreneur eleven times in a quiz during his freshman year.

His spelling had not improved much. He cheated on the spelling part of his refresher English finals. That was the only time he cheated while a student at the University of South Dakota. Joe missed out on phonics in grade school and never made up for that in high school. Unqualified high school teachers during WWII and his dad holding him out of school in the fall and spring to work on the farm caused shortcomings in his education he had yet to overcome.

Joe walked into the dean's office and stood in front of him and asked, "Should I take a class in sociology for my three-hour elective this semester?" The dean said, "Sociology should not be taught in a school of learning like this." He pointed over past the law school building and said, "Go over to the philosophy department and learn how to think." Joe said, "Okay." He stepped out of the dean's office with a slight swagger in his walk. The dean probably didn't remember him, but he suspected that the secretary did. She gave him a smile as he departed from the dean's office. Joe was still wearing the OD 33 pile Army jacket. The crew haircut and his military demeanor were things of the past. He finally had become a regular student with no hang-ups.

Joe made the Dean's Honor Roll the first semester in his junior year. His counselor during his freshman year had told him that he was a miracle student. He said to Joe, "We didn't think you would make it past the first semester." Making the Dean's Honor Roll brought invitations from two fraternities and an organization called Independents. Joe declined the fraternities politely. Debbie, the president of the Independents, invited him to a dance. Joe happily accepted. This was his first date on campus. Debbie and Joe knew each other in passing from classes they both attended that semester. Joe knew that her invitation had to do with his making the honor roll. Debbie introduced Joe to a new dance, the jitterbug. Cathy had taught him how to waltz years before the jitterbug dance arrived. Debbie asked Joe if he was a Greek, in other words, was he affiliated with a fraternity on campus. He answered, "No. I am of German-Russian descent." Unflinchingly, she asked, "I would like for you to join the Independents." He asked her, "What are the Independents?" She explained that it was an organization for students who were not in a sorority or fraternity. Joe thoughtlessly said to this nice, polite girl, "I already belong to a very exclusive fraternity." "What fraternity is that?" He said, "Joe Schultz. That's me. I am the only member." That was Joe's first and last date at the university.

Joe sloughed through his senior year pulling a "C" grade average. School had become a bore. His mother wanted him to enter law school, but Joe knew better. He didn't have the necessary reading and comprehension abilities to make it through law school. He barely passed two semesters of business law because he never got the hang of doing legal briefs. The professor heading up the school of business graduate program asked him and J.B. Brown if they were interested in getting a masters degree in business administration. Joe said to the professor, "A master's degree prepares a person better to work for someone else. I want to go into business for myself, and I don't need a master's degree for that." His friend J.B. echoed a similar answer. The professor acknowledged the two veterans' answers without rebuttal. After graduation Joe drove home, repacked his suitcases and drove to Denver. He had great expectations of making it big in real estate in the city of Denver.

Chapter XIV

In Denver, Joe rented an apartment in the Colorado University Hospital area. He made the rounds, calling on several real estate firms asking them to sponsor him for a Colorado real estate license. Nobody would sign him on. He was running low on money, so he took a job at a Conoco gas station. He wasn't the only college graduate pumping gas or working as a janitor waiting to hire on to a first post-college job. He could have interviewed with the J. C. Penney Company who had courted him before he graduated from the University of South Dakota, but he decided to stay with his plan to go into business for himself.

He met Charles, a real estate salesman, at the College Inn, a singles bar, located within walking distance from his apartment. After many beers over several weeks, Joe asked Charles to have his real estate firm sponsor him for a Colorado real estate license. Charles told him if he bought real estate through his firm he would talk to his broker about it. Charles had four sets of duplexes listed in the neighborhood for sale.

Joe was tired of smelling like a grease monkey from pumping gas at the Conoco station and not being part of the business world. The gas station job was intended to be a means to another level in life, and not an end in itself. Joe drove back to South Dakota to borrow money from his mother.

Joe told the family about his failure in Denver. They were sorry to hear about his struggle trying to establish himself in the real estate business. Gertrude offered to lend him money for a down payment on two duplexes. Cathy intervened and said, "Johnny and I want to buy your interest in the land Grandma Schultz left to you and me." Joe looked surprised and said, "I forgot about that. Dad took title to the land." Gertrude said, "Grandma's land belongs to you and Cathy." Johnny said that he and Cathy had been planning on buying out his interest for some time. Joe returned to Denver with enough money for a down payment on four duplexes and money to support himself for one year.

When he arrived in Denver with a big check in his pocket, he went to the College Inn for a meal of corned beef and sauerkraut. When Charles came in for his evening round of draft beers, Joe told him that he had the money to buy two duplexes. Subsequently, Joe bought his first two pieces of property in Denver and was sponsored by Charles's real estate firm for the real estate license. Joe kept on working at the gas station until he passed the examination. His difficulty in obtaining a real estate license was a wake-up call. Times were good in the '50s but challenges remained.

As the years went by, Joe added four twelve-unit apartment buildings to his rental properties in the Capitol Hill inner city Denver neighborhood. He wasn't getting rich but was acquiring lots of property. Commissions from real estate sales provided for his living expenses. He reinvested all profits from the rental property into upgrading them. His apartment buildings were old and needed maintenance constantly. Upkeep costs were a drain on his cash flow.

Joe had become a workaholic working seven days a week. He spent his weekends repairing, renting and cleaning up vacated apartments. During the week, he devoted his time to listing and showing property for sale. One morning when he was shaving, he saw himself in the mirror as an aging man who looked like his dad. That shook him up. Joe worked hard to become a landlord. He came to realize that the property he owned had a shortcoming. The property owned him body and soul.

He had to change his life. Joe joined the Denver Tennis Club and signed up for tennis lessons. Through his tennis playing, he met a builder who was looking for a real estate broker to assist him in finding investors for apartment buildings that he built. Joe was prepared for this challenge. He had become a broker years ago with the intention of opening his own office. Joe signed on with the apartment builder and listed his properties for sale with his real estate friend, Charles. When he signed the last contract on his property, he decided to go home and hunt pheasants. He had not been to what he still called home, South Dakota.

He drove out to Stapleton Airport, parked his car and bought a ticket to Aberdeen. He checked his suitcase and with shotgun in hand boarded the plane to Aberdeen. He slid the shotgun, in a soft carrying case, under the seat and ordered a Scotch on the rocks. The stewardess brought him the drink and a small complimentary pack of Pall Mall cigarettes. She said he was not allowed to smoke his pipe on the plane. In Rapid City, he transferred to a plane that had a goose painted on the tail. He was back in South Dakota again.

Cathy, her two boys and Gertrude were waiting for him at the airport. On the trip from Aberdeen to Hosmer, Cathy chattered about local news as she motored along the highway. Gertrude chimed in to affirm Cathy's remarks. Cathy enumerated the changes that had taken place on the farm and in Hosmer since Joe's last visit. Cathy had written to Joe about events that took place in Hosmer but skipped minor details. She had told him that Gertrude bought a small house in town and that she and Johnny built a new house in Hosmer. They moved to town so her boys could walk to school.

Johnny didn't show up at the airport to greet Joe because he had to work at the Hoffman farm, the headquarters of the family operation. The following day, Joe and his two nephews, Mike and Jay Hoffman, drove out to the Schultz farm. A visit to the farm brought back memories of his youth. He was in complete awe as they drove into the farmyard. The windmill's tail hung down, some blades of wheel were missing. Joe asked the boys, "What happened to the cow barn?" Mike, the oldest, said, "The wind blew it down. We took it apart and Dad is going to sell it as old barnwood to a guy from Colorado." Mike pointed north to the thrashing machine and said, "The guy is going to buy some of our old machinery. They are antiques." The Case thrashing machine was still parked north of Sam's grave. Joe motioned toward the thrashing machine and said, "I want to walk up to Sam's grave." Jay, the younger of the two boys, said, "Oh! Yeah, I know where that is." The grave between a small rock pile and the thrashing machine had some rocks piled at the head. Mike said, "We and Mom put those rocks around that big rock. She said you put that rock here to mark Sam's grave." The ground had shrunk down, leaving an outline of the grave. Walking back to the car, they spooked a pheasant rooster in bushes along the north fence line of the farmyard behind the chicken coop. Joe said to the boys, "There always was a family of pheasants living here as long as I can remember. Your grandma used to let hens nest down here and hatch their chicks. I found pheasants' nests in those lilacs." Joe said to the boys, "I want to see the sun set from over there." The boys followed him to the west side where the summer kitchen once was. Watching the sunset on the horizon a mile away on Schultz land reminded Joe of the time he and Cathy watched a sunset with their dad back in 1936. They saw their father cry in despair. That was the only time Joe saw his dad cry. Carl had seeded by hand about two acres in wheat around a lake to see if he could grow a few bushels. There was enough snowmelt to start the wheat. When it grew two inches tall, the heat burned some of it and the grasshoppers chewed the rest down to the roots in the ground. Carl lost all faith and wanted to end his life. Those difficult times were indelibly imprinted on Joe's mind. Many people who lived in the Dust Bowl carried scars of the Dirty Thirties with them to their graves. Joe said to the teenaged boys, "Let's go to town." Jay said, "Yeah, I am hungry."

* * * * *

Hosmer had changed from Joe's high school days. His former classmates moved away just like he did. There were fewer and fewer farms around shrinking towns. Old folks died and the younger generation moved away. Joe and Gertrude took a look around town in her Chevrolet. She suggested Joe drive to the senior citizens' home. One old fellow, who had lived at the home for many years, spoke up and said, "You are the one who left Pup here. Your mother reminds us every now and then." The old man jolted Joe. He had all but forgotten about Cathy's worthless dog. Joe, not thinking of the years that had passed by, asked, "Where is Pup?" The old man pointed to the north of the home across an open lawn and said, "He is buried back there. There is a cross to mark the grave." Joe walked out and took a look at the wooden cross bearing Pup's name. Gertrude enjoyed showing off her son to everyone in the home. Joe had a difficult time getting her to leave.

Joe stayed at his mother's house. He had to or she would have been very upset. The family spent most of their time at the Hoffman house, where they discussed everything in open forum. Gertrude directly asked Joe when he was going to get married. He said, "Probably never." She kept up with determination, "You have finished college, and making lots of money. You should have a wife and children." Joe hemmed and hawed until he moved the conversation away from marriage. Gertrude asked Joe what church he belonged to. He said, "I haven't been to church in ten years." Gertrude reprimanded him by saying, "My God. If you die we can't bury you like a dog. I stopped paying your church dues years ago. You have to belong to a church." Cathy said to Joe, "The elders of the German Reformed Church told the congregation that if they don't pay their dues on time, they will lose their membership, and if they aren't active members of the church, they can't be buried by the minister." Cathy's explanation for their mom's fears was old hat to Joe. The very reason that Joe didn't go to church was because of disgusting experiences he had had with the German Reformed minister as a young man. Joe abated the subject of church membership by turning on the TV for the evening newscast.

Joe joined Johnny for the pheasant hunt at the Hoffman farm. The Hoffman brothers planted corn and sorghum around sloughs and small water holes. In addition to feed plots, they also planted trees around the sloughs as a shelterbelt for wild game. Pheasants abounded on the farm and the deer were fat and plentiful. The Schultz farm was home to very few pheasants because they didn't have shelter or food during the winter months. Predators almost drove the pheasant to extinction on the prairies.

At the end of the day, they cleaned the birds in what was the farm slaughterhouse. The Hoffmans butchered their hogs, steers and deer next to a meat preparation area in the barn. They cut up the hogs and steers and made their sausages in this room. Next to the barn was a sizeable smokehouse. Everything on the farm was big enough to serve two generations of Hoffmans.

The open spaces in South Dakota made Joe realize how noisy, smoggy and congested Denver really was. In the big city, he struggled with street traffic and stood in line wherever he went to eat or shop. On the day he left to board his flight in Aberdeen for Denver, he teasingly said that he would move back to South Dakota. That excited his mother. He said, "On second thought, I better stay in Denver a few more years. Have to make a living." He was staying in Denver for the same reasons he went there in the first place, to make money. He lived in an apartment in Denver that he never called home. It was only an apartment to him. Colorado was the place where he made a good living. Home was the Schultz farm in South Dakota.

Joe left the shotgun at his mother's house. The Hoffman farm was the only place he would ever hunt pheasants, ducks and geese. At the airport in Aberdeen, he checked in a suitcase and a Styrofoam container with Dakota goodies: two pheasants, four smoked summer sausages and four pork fry sausages from the Hoffman farm and a couple of kuchen his mother had baked for him.

Chapter XV

The plane flew Joe across South Dakota, landing at Pierre and Rapid City, and then on to Denver. The stops at Pierre and Rapid City were abbreviated landings. The pilot shut down the left engine, allowing passengers to deplane and board the plane while the right engine churned. In Denver, he drove his Corvette to his apartment complex and put away the sausages, pheasants and kuchen.

Joe's life followed the same routine for years thereafter. He was involved with two different builders arranging financing and selling partnerships in apartment buildings. In the winter months, he skied every weekend and in the summer months played tennis with the same intensity. His social life was a series of occasional affairs that lasted from one weekend to one season. His mother stopped bugging him about getting married. She gave up on that idea. He kept making trips back to South Dakota, skipping a year or two between visits. Joe now was in his early sixties and his social life was reduced to living alone. He never was a social animal, quite the opposite. On a beautiful fall day, Cathy called him and told him to take a flight to Aberdeen the next day. Gertrude, their mother, had died. Her heart gave out.

She had told Cathy the day before she died that it was time for her to go into the other world. She said that her work on earth was finished, and the next morning she died.

Joe was shaken by his mother's death. He should have been happy to see his mother pass away on almost her own terms. Joe always thought that his mother could see into the future. She only had a sixth-grade education but possessed phenomenal insight into people and life. Joe had a very close relationship with his sister and mother. That is all the family he ever had except for a father-son relationship that vanished in his senior year in high school.

The fifth generation of Hoffman boys, including Cathy and Johnny's two sons, were the pallbearers for Gertrude Schultz. Joe felt uneasy during his mother's funeral service at the German Reformed Church. When they lowered her into the ground next to her husband, Joe almost lost it. He had not been to his dad's grave since returning from Korea. Cathy tried to make Joe understand that their mother's death was a blessing. She said to Joe, "We all will go that way some day. Let's hope we are as healthy and mentally alert as she was to the day of her parting." Joe, out of the blue, said to Cathy, "Do me a favor. When I die, sprinkle my ashes over Sam's grave at our farm." Cathy was perplexed at Joe's out-of-context comment. She let it pass. Cathy fixed a big supper for all those who cared to share it with her.

Joe's nephews energized him and lifted his spirits. Mike had graduated from the university with a degree in business and Jay had an engineering degree from South Dakota State. Mike and Jay were the only two Hoffman boys who didn't farm. In many ways, they took after their Uncle Joe. The next day, Joe decided to satisfy nostalgia of his past life on the prairie, specifically the Schultz farm.

He drove up to the German Reformed country church that the family traveled to on a sled, in a buggy or the Model T truck in the thirties. Tall grass blocked out the church foundation, two outhouse pits and a small graveyard where his great grandparents and grandparents were buried. Across to the east of the former church site were remnants of a farm that Gertrude was born and raised on. He drove down the road passing foundations for buildings that once made up his uncle's farm that he abandoned and left for California during the Depression. On the road back to the Schultz farm he stopped at the site were the country schoolhouse once stood. Years ago he and Cathy rode Sam to this school. The cement base for the flagpole that he climbed many times was still there. He found two dips marking where the boys and girls' outhouse used to set. He drove a mile west and turned south on a road that his dad with a team had worked for the WPA. By now the hills had been leveled off and the roadbed across lakes and sloughs was elevated. The road was paved. Their mailbox used to be on the corner he had turned south on until Hillsview ceased to be a town. A mile south, he turned into what was left of the Schultz farm. The granary and outhouse were the only original buildings left. Johnny

Hoffman's Butler machine was next to where the garage and blacksmith shop were before they burned down.

Joe reminisced about the sodbusters that should have left the prairies as God had created them. The land around the Schultz farm never was very productive and busting the grasslands was a mistake. If it had not been for government subsidies, most of the farmland would have reverted to grassland years ago. Farmers in McPherson County for the most part had been on federal welfare rolls for decades. Welfare had become a way of life for them since the Dirty Thirties.

Joe walked to the north of the farmyard looking for the rock pile next to Sam's grave. It was gone. Johnny had taken heavy equipment and dug trenches to bury rock piles that were started by Joe's great grandfather and added to by every generation thereafter. Farmers put the rocks back were they came from, in the ground. Joe did locate an outcropping where the rock pile had been. All the old machinery was gone. Like his nephews said, "Dad is going to sell the barnwood and antiques to a guy in Colorado." Joe imagined the old cow barn wood gracing the inside of a franchised fastfood restaurant with great grandfather's sod-busting plow on a roof next to a food chain's sign. Joe located what appeared to be indentations on the ground outlining Sam's grave. He walked back to the center of the farmyard. The windmill was gone. Johnny had bulldozed all the foundations of the farm buildings and buried them except for the house foundation.

The old cottonwood tree that shaded the cattle water tank and windmill was still there, but dying.

Joe walked to the spot where he and Cathy years ago watched their dad cry as he watched the sun set. The sun turned a red and orange color as it dipped behind the horizon. The Dakota sky turned a deep blue. Joe whispered to himself, "God, I do miss this place. This is home and always will be home."

ISBN 141203566-X